The Silent ~~Suspect~~

Nancy took a step forward into the crowd on the tower's observation deck. "Richard!" she called.

He spun around at the sound of his name, terror in his eyes. Then he darted toward the stairway. But just then, a group of kids came rushing up the stairs and blocked his way.

That gave Nancy the few seconds she needed to catch up to Richard. She reached out and grabbed his arm—just as he started headlong down the stairs.

"Nancy, watch out!" Ned yelled.

It was too late. Nancy had already lost her balance at the edge of the stairs. In the next instant, she had the eerie feeling that she was flying through space.

The only sound she heard was her own scream of fear.

Nancy Drew Mystery Stories

Available from MINSTREL Books

NANCY DREW®

THE SILENT SUSPECT

CAROLYN KEENE

A MINSTREL® BOOK

PUBLISHED BY POCKET BOOKS

New York   London   Toronto   Sydney   Tokyo   Singapore

A MINSTREL PAPERBACK *ORIGINAL*

 A Minstrel Book, published by
POCKET BOOKS, a division of Simon & Schuster Inc.
1230 Avenue of the Americas, New York, NY 10020

ISBN: 0-671-69280-1

First Minstrel Books printing June 1990

10   9   8   7   6   5   4   3   2   1

Contents

1

Secrets in San Francisco

"Nan? Where are you?"

Nancy Drew jumped in surprise. "Ned? Is that you?" she called. "I'm out in the backyard."

Nancy sprang to her feet and brushed the dirt off the knees of her jeans. She smoothed back her reddish blond hair just as her longtime boyfriend, Ned Nickerson, walked around the corner of her house. A big grin spread across his face when he saw her.

"Surprise!" Ned called. He picked Nancy up and spun her around in a huge hug. Then he set her back on her feet.

"It's a *terrific* surprise!" she told him happily. Her blue eyes sparkled. "But I thought your spring break starts tomorrow."

"It does," Ned answered. "But I had only one class this morning so I left school a day early to

1

come see you. Besides," he added teasingly, "I wouldn't miss a chance to catch my favorite girl with mud on her face."

Nancy blushed and lifted a hand to wipe off her cheek.

"Seriously, Nan," Ned said, "something important has come up. I have a problem, and I thought you could help me." Suddenly his brown eyes looked anxious.

Nancy was used to helping people. Although she was only eighteen, she'd been an amateur detective for years, and she'd solved dozens of cases. "Come on inside while I clean up," she told Ned. "We can have some iced tea while you tell me all about it."

A few minutes later Nancy and Ned were sitting at the big table in the Drews' cheerful kitchen. Hannah Gruen, the Drews' housekeeper, set a pitcher of iced tea and a plate of fresh-baked chocolate-chip cookies on the table in front of them. Hannah had lived with the family ever since Nancy's mother had died, when Nancy was three years old.

"Thanks, Hannah," Nancy said with a smile. "Those cookies look delicious."

"They *are* delicious," said Ned, taking a large bite.

Nancy turned back to her boyfriend as Hannah

2

left the kitchen. "Tell me about the problem, Ned," she said eagerly. "Is it some kind of mystery?"

"No, not really," Ned answered. "It's more of a personal problem. Do you remember my cousin Lisa Franklin?"

Nancy thought for a minute, then nodded. "I think so," she said slowly. "I met her once when her family visited River Heights. She's about my age, isn't she? From San Francisco? And she's got a sister, Laurel, who's a little older?"

"That's right," Ned told her.

"Lisa was nice," Nancy said, remembering. "Very smart and fun to be with. I liked her a lot."

Ned's expression was grim. "Lisa *was* fun to be with," he said. "Really bubbly, always giggling about something. But that seems to have changed now. Her dad—my uncle Bob—phoned me the other day. He said there's something really wrong with Lisa. She's completely changed, he told me. She won't talk to him. She won't spend any more time at home than she absolutely has to. Uncle Bob thinks she's hiding something."

"Did he tell you what he thinks it is?" Nancy asked.

Ned shook his head. "He wouldn't say anything more on the phone. But he's worried enough that he asked me to fly out to San Francisco to try to help. Lisa and I were big pals when we were growing up. I'm the only cousin she has."

"I see," said Nancy thoughtfully. "And you thought I might be able to help, too?"

"Well, yes," Ned admitted. "Would you mind, Nancy? Maybe Lisa just needs to talk to another girl her own age. After all, Lisa's mother died when Lisa and Laurel were very young. Maybe whatever's bothering Lisa is something she can't talk about with her dad. Or with me," Ned added. "Anyway, I'd hate to have Uncle Bob fly me all the way out there and then not be able to help him. With you along, I'm sure we could solve the problem."

"I'd love to come," said Nancy with a smile. "But why can't Lisa's sister try to help her?"

"Well, that's another thing," Ned said. "Uncle Bob says Lisa won't talk to Laurel, either. In fact, the way he put it, it almost sounds as if Lisa isn't speaking to her family at all. And that's *really* weird. Lisa and Laurel have always been more like best friends than sisters." He shook his head. "I just don't understand what's going on."

Nancy frowned and took a sip of her iced tea. "Well, you're wrong about one thing, Ned," she told him. "This *is* a mystery."

"Then you'll help?" asked Ned.

"I told you, I'd love to! Besides, things have been way too quiet around here lately. I'll have to check

4

with Dad, of course, but I think a trip to San Francisco is just what I need."

"Great," Ned said happily. "And I'm sure we'll have plenty of time to go sight-seeing, too."

"We'd better," Nancy teased. "San Francisco is one of the most romantic cities in the world. I don't want to spend *all* my time being a detective."

The late-afternoon sun was low in the sky as Nancy and Ned's plane began its descent into San Francisco's international airport. Gazing out of the airplane window, Nancy could see the graceful curves of the Golden Gate Bridge. The sun was sparkling on the water of the bay below.

"It looks beautiful," she told Ned. "What a great place for a case."

Ned and Nancy had just picked up their suitcases in the baggage claim area when a thin man in his thirties approached them. He had wiry brown hair and horn-rimmed glasses, and he was wearing a conservative blue blazer and gray flannel pants.

"Excuse me," the man said. "Are you, by any chance, Ms. Drew and Mr. Nickerson?"

"Yes, we are," Nancy answered for both of them.

The man broke into a wide grin. "Great," he said, sounding relieved. "I'm Christopher Toomey. I work for Mr. Franklin. He sent me to pick you up."

5

"That was nice of him," Nancy said, smiling back.

"I see you have your bags already," Mr. Toomey said. "We'll be in time for dinner, then. Mr. Franklin likes everyone to be on time for meals," he added, bending to pick up their suitcases.

"Oh, that's okay," said Ned quickly. "We can carry—"

"It's my pleasure," said Mr. Toomey. "We want you to feel welcome here." Suitcases in hand, he led Ned and Nancy toward a long walkway. "Parking's in this direction," he said over his shoulder. "I'm right at the curb."

Christopher Toomey led them up to a gleaming black Lincoln and opened the trunk. As he stacked their suitcases inside, Ned asked, "Are you having dinner with us, too?"

"Oh, yes." Mr. Toomey shrugged. "I almost always have dinner with the Franklins. I'm practically one of the family. I'm very important to the firm, you see."

He bustled to the car's back door and opened it with a flourish. Nancy and Ned exchanged an amused look as they climbed in. Mr. Toomey certainly *thinks* he's important, anyway! Nancy said to herself. But he did seem very nice.

"I didn't realize Uncle Bob had a partner," Ned said pleasantly as they pulled away from the curb.

6

Mr. Toomey's face flushed. "Well, I'm not a partner, exactly," he said. "But it's just myself and Laurel working with Mr. Franklin in his office. Both of us are quite valuable to Mr. Franklin."

"I see," said Nancy. She didn't dare look over at Ned. "I didn't know Laurel was already an architect."

Mr. Toomey nodded. "She received her degree last year. She's only twenty-four, but she worked very hard and finished school a year early." He paused. "Lisa is supposed to do the same thing."

Nancy sat up straighter. This was the first time Lisa's name had been mentioned. Maybe Mr. Toomey could shed some light on Lisa's character. After all, he had probably seen Lisa quite often. Sometimes people outside a family noticed things that family members didn't.

"Lisa must be very smart," Nancy remarked casually.

"She skipped several grades in school," Ned answered. "She's only nineteen, but she's already a college senior. She's a real whiz in math. After Lisa graduates from college, she'll go to architecture school. In the meantime she works for her dad whenever she can. Uncle Bob told me Lisa's at the firm on weekends and during vacations."

"That doesn't leave her much time for fun, does it?" asked Nancy.

"Fun!" Christopher Toomey snorted. "She doesn't have time for fun! Mr. Franklin has a very successful business. Lisa is going to run it someday. She's *got* to work hard!"

"Wait a minute," Nancy said. "What about Laurel? She's older, and she's already working for Mr. Franklin. Wouldn't Laurel run the business?"

Mr. Toomey shrugged. "Lisa is her father's favorite," he said, frowning as he edged the car into the freeway traffic.

Hmm, Nancy thought. It sounds as though there may be a family problem. Does that have anything to do with Lisa's acting so strangely?

Nancy turned and stared out the car window. Beyond the freeway San Francisco Bay glittered in the late-afternoon sunshine. The car took them past gleaming white stucco houses surrounded by palm trees and tropical plants. When Mr. Toomey took an exit into the city of San Francisco itself, the streets became quite narrow. The car climbed one steep hill after another, rising and plunging abruptly. At the end of each street Nancy could see past rooftops to the bay.

"This is beautiful!" Nancy exclaimed.

Ned grinned. "I arranged it all for you," he murmured.

After about ten minutes of driving, they turned onto a narrow street where the houses were large and set back on broad, manicured lawns. Most of the houses were surrounded by bright tropical flowers and spiky green plants that Nancy recognized as yuccas.

Mr. Toomey pulled the car into a steep driveway that led up a hill. Soon Nancy saw a large white house with a red tile roof and whitewashed stucco walls. Its windows had black wrought-iron grilles covered with green ivy.

"Here we are," Mr. Toomey announced. "I'll take you in right away and get your bags later. Mr. Franklin is waiting."

A middle-aged woman with gray hair met them at the front door. "I'm Mrs. Truitt, the Franklins' housekeeper," she said with a warm smile. "I'd be happy to help you unpack later, if you'd like. If there's anything you need, please let me know."

"Thank you, Mrs. Truitt," said Nancy. "That's very nice of you."

"I think Mr. Franklin is expecting Nancy and Ned in the living room," Mr. Toomey broke in.

Mrs. Truitt nodded. "Of course."

Mr. Toomey led Nancy and Ned across the hallway and into a huge living room. It was a handsome room, with Oriental rugs on the floor, white furniture, and a gleaming grand piano at one end. But somehow the room was so formal that it looked to Nancy as if no one ever used it. Even the needlepoint pillows on the sofa were lined up in precise rows.

Mr. Franklin had been standing by the piano. Now he turned to greet them, extending a hand to Ned. "Glad you could make it, Ned," he said. "It's good to see you again." His voice sounded polite but cold, Nancy thought, not very welcoming at all.

Robert Franklin was about fifty, with gray hair and steel blue eyes that looked piercingly at Nancy as Ned introduced her.

"I'm happy to meet you, Nancy," he said, giving her a firm handshake. "Why don't the two of you sit down?"

"I'll go ask Mrs. Truitt for some iced tea," said Mr. Toomey. He headed quickly out toward the kitchen.

"My daughters are still at the office," said Mr. Franklin. "They'll join us later on."

"Lisa's working already?" Ned asked, surprised.

"Her semester break started today," Mr. Franklin told him. "I made sure she got right to work."

Some vacation! Nancy thought. Aloud, she asked, "What exactly do Lisa and Laurel do at the office, Mr. Franklin?"

"Well, Laurel's working on the design of a major project of mine," Mr. Franklin told her. "Lisa is supposed to be helping her." He sighed. "But I'm afraid she won't be much help the way things are going." He broke off as Mr. Toomey came in, carrying a tray with a pitcher and several glasses. "Thanks, Christopher. Just put that on the coffee table," Mr. Franklin said. He turned back to Nancy and Ned as Mr. Toomey sat down.

"So things aren't getting better?" Ned asked.

Mr. Franklin sighed again. "I just don't know what's wrong with Lisa. She isn't herself at all. I certainly hope you two can find out what's bothering her."

"We'll try," said Nancy. "Does Lisa work at the office every weekend, Mr. Franklin?"

"That's right," he answered. "During the week she stays in the dorm at college. She's at San Rafael University, about thirty miles north of here."

"That's where Uncle Bob went to school," Ned told Nancy.

"It's a fine school," said Mr. Franklin. "San Rafael has one of the best architecture departments in the country. Laurel went there also, so you might say Lisa's following in the family tradition." Mr. Franklin frowned. "She should be grateful. It's a wonderful opportunity. Instead, she's got this crazy idea of dropping out!"

He fixed his gaze on Ned. "That's one of the main reasons I've asked you here," he said. "I want you to make sure Lisa stays in school. I'll be frank with you, Ned. I'm a very busy man. I don't have time for

11

all this nonsense. Lisa works for me only part-time, and she has a lot to learn. But someday she's going to be a talented architect. I can't let anything, or anyone, interfere with that."

He sounds as though the only problem with Lisa is that she's standing in the way of his plans, Nancy thought. He doesn't seem worried about Lisa's feelings at all. Maybe—

Just then a car screeched to a halt outside the house. There was the sound of a car door slamming. Then the tires screeched again as the car sped away. In the front hall the door banged open and shut.

A young woman appeared in the living room doorway. She was wearing a short black skirt and a black-and-white T-shirt. She was Nancy's height and very slender, with dark, wavy hair cut short to frame her pretty face. But right now that face was flushed and angry-looking. The young woman's brown eyes were bright with hostility as she surveyed the group in the living room.

"Lisa!" said Mr. Franklin in surprise. "I thought you were working late tonight. Did something go wrong at the office?"

Lisa Franklin gave her father a sullen look. "I'm not home early," she said. "I *quit*. I hate that office, and I'm never going back to work there again. Not for the rest of my life!"

12

2

Threats and Tears

There was a shocked silence in the living room. Lisa threw her briefcase onto the sofa and turned to walk away.

"Now, wait just a minute, young lady!" said her father sternly. "What's all this talk about quitting. A Franklin never quits."

For a second Lisa's eyes met Nancy's. To Nancy's surprise, the other girl looked worried—almost afraid.

"Lisa, I'm speaking to you," Mr. Franklin said. It sounded like a warning.

Lisa remained silent. She opened her mouth, but closed it on whatever she'd been about to say. Then, bursting into tears, she dashed from the room. A moment later Nancy heard Lisa running up the stairs.

"Now you can see what I'm talking about!" Mr. Franklin told Ned angrily.

"I, uh, sure do," said Ned. "Uncle Bob, would it be okay if I went up and tried to talk to her?"

Mr. Franklin sighed. "Go ahead. I'm sure you'll have better luck than I did."

With a quick smile to Nancy, Ned crossed the room and headed upstairs.

"This whole thing couldn't have come at a worse time," said Mr. Franklin. "I happen to be working on a very big project right now. It's an expensive condominium complex called Franklin Place. Lisa will learn a lot by working on this project. She simply can't quit!"

Mr. Franklin was starting to sound awfully selfish to Nancy. She leaned forward and asked politely, "Excuse me for asking, Mr. Franklin, but have you ever asked Lisa if she *likes* working so much?"

Mr. Toomey glanced uncomfortably at his boss. Mr. Franklin's answer came immediately.

"There's no need to ask her a question like that," he said. "I've always dreamed of having both my daughters in the firm with me, but especially Lisa. Besides, I worked twice as hard when I was Lisa's age."

Nancy gave him a friendly smile. "Maybe Lisa doesn't want to quit completely," she said gently.

"Maybe she just needs some time to make up her own mind about her future."

Mr. Franklin glared at Nancy. "Ms. Drew, that kind of suggestion isn't very useful. I'm delighted to have you here helping Ned—*if* you're going to help him. But speculating about things you can't possibly understand . . ." His voice trailed away.

Finally, Mr. Franklin continued. "I'm a busy man, but Lisa has always had everything she wanted. She has no reason for grievances. Why, I—"

To Nancy's relief, Ned walked back into the room just then. "No luck," he said, shaking his head. "I tried, Uncle Bob, but she wouldn't even open her door. Maybe *you'll* be able to get somewhere, Nancy."

"We'll see about that," said Mr. Franklin. Abruptly, he stood up. "I'll call Mrs. Truitt to show you to your rooms," he said.

"I'd be glad to do that," Mr. Toomey put in quickly.

For just a moment Mr. Franklin seemed to relax. "That's very considerate, Christopher," he said with a slight nod as the younger man left the room. Then he turned back to Ned and Nancy. "Ned, you'll stay in the guest room. Nancy, I'm afraid the other spare bed is in Lisa's room. Anyway, you'll get

15

a chance to ask her all the questions you want. Whether she'll answer them, I don't know."

"Thanks, Uncle Bob," Ned said quickly. "I'm sure that will work out fine." He beckoned Nancy to follow him out into the hall, where Mr. Toomey was entering with their suitcases. The two of them followed Mr. Toomey up the stairs.

Ned put his hand on Nancy's arm as they reached the top. "Sorry about Uncle Bob," he said quietly. "He sounded as though he was being pretty rude to you."

"He seems like the type who's rude to everyone," Nancy said with a shrug. "I didn't take it personally. But I *do* feel a little sorry for Lisa."

Ned squeezed her hand. "I feel sorry for her, too. But I have a feeling she's not going to make things easy on you. It's too bad you have to share her room."

"I'm not worried," Nancy said. "I'm sure we'll get along fine."

And even if we don't, she thought, sharing a room with Lisa will help me find out more about her, whether she wants me to or not.

Mr. Toomey was waiting for them halfway down the hall. "Here's your bedroom, Nancy," he said. "Ned, yours is at the end of the hall."

"Okay," said Ned. "I'll unpack and meet you

16

downstairs for dinner, okay, Nan?" He smiled encouragingly at her.

"Sure thing," Nancy said, smiling back.

Lisa's door was closed. Nancy tapped lightly, but there was no answer. She turned the knob and pushed the door open a crack. The room was empty.

One of the beds inside was unmade and rumpled. Nancy put her suitcase on the other bed and began to unpack. Now and then she glanced around the room.

The room didn't give her many clues about Lisa's personality. The room was decorated in soft shades of rose and ivory, with watercolor prints of famous cathedrals on the walls. The top of Lisa's bureau was bare, but her desk was covered with neat stacks of drawing paper, pens, and drawing tools. The wide bookcase extending across one wall was filled almost entirely with books about architecture.

Hmm, thought Nancy. All work and no play. But somehow, even the brief glimpse she'd had of Lisa didn't fit that description. And hadn't Ned told her that his cousin had been a lot of fun before she'd started acting so strangely?

Nancy washed her face quickly in the bathroom that adjoined Lisa's bedroom. Then she changed into fresh clothes and brushed her hair. It was almost dinnertime, and Mr. Toomey had said that Mr. Franklin hated people being late to dinner.

Ned was just leaving his room as Nancy walked out into the hall. "Any luck?" he asked in a low voice.

Nancy shook her head. "Lisa's not there, Ned. I don't know where she went. I'm sure I'll get a chance to talk to her before bedtime, though."

"I'm wondering whether Laurel comes into this at all," Ned said as they started downstairs. "I never noticed before how Uncle Bob seems to favor Lisa. Don't you think that would drive Laurel crazy?"

"Maybe," Nancy replied. "But I don't want to make any assumptions about Laurel before I've met her. Anyway, even if Laurel is jealous, that doesn't explain why Lisa's so upset."

"Well, we've got lots of time to work things out," said Ned. "Besides, I'm starving. That snack they gave us on the plane seems an awfully long time ago."

When they reached the dining room, Nancy was startled to see that it was set for a formal dinner. Gold-rimmed plates, heavy silverware, and sterling candlesticks were lined up with absolute precision on the white tablecloth. A massive flower arrangement sat in the exact center of the table. Above it hung a brass chandelier that was so ornate and heavy-looking that Nancy couldn't help worrying that it might crash down on the table.

Mr. Franklin was already standing at the head of the table. There was a look of slight disapproval on his face, as though he resented having been kept waiting for even a few seconds. Mr. Toomey was standing at a place farther down the table. And across from Mr. Franklin stood a serious-looking young woman in a blue dress.

"Hi, Laurel!" said Ned, crossing the room to kiss her. "It's great to see you again!"

Laurel gave him a strained, anxious smile. "It's nice to see you, too," she said.

Nancy noticed the young woman's resemblance to Lisa. Everything about Laurel, however, seemed more subdued. Her hair was a mousier shade of brown, and it was straight instead of curly. She was paler than her sister, and her clothes looked prim and out of style. Laurel kept glancing timidly at her father as though she were waiting for his approval.

Ned smiled warmly at Nancy. "Remember Nancy Drew, Laurel?" he asked. "You met her back in River Heights."

"Oh, yes," said Laurel faintly, nodding in Nancy's direction.

That was all. There was an awkward pause, which Nancy finally broke. "Well, I can hardly wait to see more of San Francisco," she said. "It looked great from the car."

This time Laurel's eyes lit up. "Oh, it is," she said. "We have some of the finest architecture in the country."

Mr. Franklin looked impatiently at his watch. "Where's Lisa?" he asked with a frown. "She's late."

Laurel gave him another one of her nervous glances. "Why don't we all sit down, Dad?" she suggested. "I—I'm sure Lisa will be here in a minute."

"Oh, all right," answered her father in a disgruntled voice. He pulled out his chair and sat down. The rest of the table followed suit. Then a second tense pause fell across the room as everyone tried to think of something to say.

Well, this certainly isn't one big happy family, Nancy thought. Mr. Franklin was so stern, Laurel was nervous, and Lisa so angry. She didn't understand exactly where Christopher Toomey fit in. What did he make of all this?

Mr. Franklin cleared his throat. "Go upstairs and find your sister, please," he told Laurel. "Tell her that—"

20

"I'm here," came a sullen voice from the doorway.

Everyone looked up as Lisa entered the dining room and took her seat.

Lisa had changed her casual skirt and T-shirt for black leggings, black boots, a black turtleneck, and an oversize black jacket. On Lisa's wrist was a single gold bracelet. The wide, curved band caught the light from the chandelier as Lisa flicked her napkin off the table.

Nancy smiled at Lisa. "That's a really nice outfit," she said.

Lisa stared at her plate in reply. Nancy saw that her eyes were still red.

"Where are your manners, Lisa?" asked Mr. Franklin angrily. "You just received a compliment!"

"Oh, that's okay," said Nancy quickly. She didn't want to make Lisa more upset than she already was. She had a feeling it would only make Lisa close up even more.

Suddenly Laurel spoke up. "It *isn't* okay!" she said hotly. "Lisa's acting like a spoiled brat. All she does is mope around, and she gets away with it!"

Lisa turned to her sister. "I'm surprised you even notice!" she flared. "You never pay any attention to me!"

21

"That's enough, girls," said Mr. Franklin sternly. "Could we just try to have a pleasant meal for once? We have guests, for heaven's sake! And that reminds me. Lisa, tomorrow you should show Ned and Nancy around Franklin Place."

Lisa jumped up so fast that she knocked over her water glass. Water streamed to the floor, but everyone was too startled to do anything about it.

"I'm not showing anybody anything," she said between clenched teeth. "I hate that place. I wish it would burn to the ground. Then you'd all be sorry!"

Before anyone could say a word, she ran from the dining room.

Mr. Franklin slapped his napkin onto the table. "Well, here we go again," he said. "Another meal ruined, courtesy of Lisa!"

Nancy walked into the bedroom with a sigh of relief. The meal itself had been wonderful, but Lisa hadn't come back, and the dinner-table conversation had never really gotten going. The end of dinner had been welcomed by everyone.

Downstairs, Mr. Franklin had just announced that coffee was going to be served in the library. Nancy had slipped upstairs for a moment to get some aspirin from her purse. Whether it was stress or just the long day she'd had, she could definitely feel the beginning of a headache coming on.

What a messed-up family, Nancy thought as she took her purse off the bed. Whatever Lisa's problem was, living in the Franklin house could only make it worse. Or maybe it was living there that was causing the problem.

Suddenly Nancy heard a sound coming from the hall. It sounded like Lisa's voice. And she sounded as if she was crying.

Nancy tiptoed to the doorway and listened for a moment. The sound was coming from the opposite end of the long hall, across from Ned's room. She walked quietly toward it.

The other two bedroom doors were open, and Nancy could see that no one was inside. She was about to give up when she noticed a telephone cord stretched across the hallway. It ran from a table standing between two of the bedrooms and around a corner at the very end of the hall. Nancy peeked around the corner and saw a small nook by a back stairway.

Lisa was curled up inside the space with her back to Nancy. She was clutching the telephone close to her mouth, and her slender shoulders were shaking with sobs beneath the black jacket. Nancy couldn't help feeling a pang of sympathy. Obviously, whatever was bothering Lisa was more than some trivial family problem.

She was turning to leave Lisa in privacy when the girl's voice suddenly rose.

"I'm telling you, he'll be sorry. I'll *make* him sorry!" she cried. "When I'm done with him, he won't even know what hit him!"

3

Fire!

Lisa slammed down the receiver, and Nancy ducked behind the guest-room door. She was just in time, too. Lisa walked swiftly down the hall toward the stairs. A few seconds later the front door slammed.

Well! Nancy thought. Lisa Franklin certainly had a dramatic way of making an exit! Did she ever just walk out of a room like an ordinary person?

Nancy headed toward the stairs herself. She hoped she'd be able to catch Ned alone in the library so she could tell him what she'd overheard.

But as she walked into the oak-paneled room lined with hundreds of books, she saw that Mr. Franklin, Laurel, and Mr. Toomey were there already. Mr. Franklin and Mr. Toomey were studying an architectural magazine. Ned looked as if he were trying to draw Laurel into conversation, but he wasn't having much luck. Laurel kept biting her lip and staring out the window.

"Nancy! There you are at last. Was Lisa upstairs?" asked Mr. Franklin, glancing up from the magazine.

"Uh—I didn't run into her," said Nancy. It wasn't exactly a lie, she thought to herself. After all, Lisa hadn't seen her.

Laurel pursed her lips. "She probably sneaked out of the house to meet her boyfriend," she said with a sidelong glance at her father.

"Her boyfriend?" echoed Nancy.

Laurel shrugged. "I wouldn't be surprised. He's always showing up when you least expect him."

"What's his name?" asked Ned.

"Richard Bates," answered Laurel. "That's all I know about him, except that Lisa met him at college. He lives in an apartment off campus. She hasn't told me anything else."

Nancy looked over at Ned. "Maybe we should talk to Richard Bates," she said. "He might know what's bothering Lisa."

"If you ask me, *he's* what's bothering her," snapped Mr. Franklin angrily. "Richard is a terrible influence on Lisa."

"In what way?" asked Nancy in surprise.

"That young man is steering her off the right path. Lisa should be studying hard and working for me, the way Laurel did. She can learn plenty while she's still in school. Even if photocopying and running errands don't seem like much to her, she'll be finding out how an architecture office works. Then, after she graduates, she'll know what to expect when she comes to work officially at the firm. She can take her place alongside Laurel, creating designs, or she can work with Christopher to oversee the building process for each project."

Doesn't Lisa get to make up her own mind about any of this? Nancy wanted to ask. But there was no point in making Mr. Franklin even angrier. "And her boyfriend keeps her from doing that?" she said aloud.

"That's right," said Mr. Franklin. "He takes her mind away from her work." He broke off as Mrs. Truitt came into the room with the coffee. "Thank you, Mrs. Truitt," he said.

The interruption seemed to have distracted him, for Mr. Franklin suddenly pulled a thick leather scrapbook from one of the bookshelves. He held the book out to Ned and Nancy. "I'd like you to see some of my work," he said proudly.

Nancy stood up to look over Ned's shoulder as Mr. Franklin slowly turned the page. Laurel and Mr. Toomey watched in silence.

The buildings in the scrapbook were all quite handsome: elegant, classical-looking structures that fit in well with their surroundings. Nancy recognized a few of the more famous buildings, but none of them seemed particularly exciting to her. She was no architect, of course, but the structures were all a bit conservative for her taste.

Once again Nancy kept her thoughts to herself. "I'm very impressed," she told Mr. Franklin. "These are just beautiful." Ned nodded in agreement.

Mr. Franklin smiled broadly—a real smile this time. "I'm glad you like them," he said. "Now take a look at my newest creation!"

He closed the scrapbook and opened an oak cabinet with wide, shallow drawers built to hold large sheets of paper. "These are copies of the plans for Franklin Place," he told Nancy and Ned, pulling out a stack of drawings. He began flipping through them, one after another.

Like Mr. Franklin's other work, the designs were solidly classical. Franklin Place, it seemed, would be a handsome apartment building that might easily have been built fifty years before. But there was no denying that it would be an attractive spot to live in.

"It's great, Uncle Bob," Ned said. "Really terrific."

"Everything's the best that money can buy," Mr. Franklin boasted.

28

Nancy caught Ned's eye and wondered if he was thinking the same thing she was: It would be nice if Mr. Franklin was as proud of his daughters as he was of Franklin Place.

"Christopher, would you mind getting out the blueprints?" Mr. Franklin asked his associate. Mr. Toomey immediately opened another drawer and lifted out a set of blueprints that showed the construction details for every floor.

Nancy had never realized how much planning went into a building. Everything in Franklin Place seemed to have been accounted for, from the wall outlets to the telephone cables.

"I'm overwhelmed!" Nancy said at last. "Designing a building is so much work."

Unexpectedly, Laurel spoke up. "It *is* a lot of work," she agreed. "But it's fun, too. I love doing the math for the calculations and designing how it will all look. And working with Dad is great." Her eyes glowed with excitement. "He's a genius. I'm learning so much."

"That's great, honey," said Mr. Franklin kindly. Then he sighed. "I only wish your sister felt the same way you do. She's going to be a brilliant success someday." He bent his head to the blueprints and began to study them.

Laurel gave a little gasp, and her face flushed scarlet. Biting her lip, she turned away from her father and began awkwardly pleating the hem of her skirt between her fingers.

Ned cleared his throat before the silence in the room became too painful. "Uh, Uncle Bob, how much of Franklin Place is already built?" he asked.

"Well, the foundation is laid," Mr. Franklin told him. "The framing's done, too, and we've got the first three floors drywalled. We're right on schedule."

"Speaking of schedules," Mr. Toomey put in, "I wonder if you might have time to go over the electrical plans with me, sir? I do have a call in to the electricians. It would be nice to—"

Mr. Franklin was already on his feet. "All right, Christopher, let's get busy," he said. He turned to Nancy, Ned, and Laurel. "Would you mind excusing us?"

That seemed to mean they should leave.

As the three of them walked out of the library, Nancy turned to Laurel. "Do you have a minute?" she asked. "Ned and I would love to talk to you."

"Sure," Laurel said. She hesitated. "But if it's about Lisa, I don't really have much to say."

"That's fine," said Nancy. "Shall we sit down in here?" She paused at the living room door.

Laurel sighed and entered the room. She sat down gingerly on the very edge of the nearest chair.

She looked uncomfortable, as if she didn't want to be there at all.

Ned gave Nancy a warning glance. Be careful, he seemed to be telling her.

Nancy did her best. "Well, I'd really like to know a little more about Richard Bates," she said pleasantly.

Laurel shrugged. At that moment she looked very much like her sister. "I already told you, I don't know much about him. But I agree with Dad—he's a bad influence on Lisa."

"Even though you don't know him?" Nancy asked gently.

Laurel stiffened.

"I was wondering if you might be a little angry at Lisa," Nancy continued quickly. She knew this was a risky topic, but she couldn't see any subtle way to bring it up.

"Why would I be?" Laurel asked, looking at the floor.

"Well, I know this is none of my business," Nancy said, keeping her tone friendly. "But if I were you, I might be a little upset that my younger sister was supposed to take over the business someday."

Laurel colored deeply. "Lisa's very smart," she told Nancy. "Even smarter than I was at her age." She leaned forward. "But I really love the architecture business. Lisa doesn't. It isn't fair that Lisa should get to run the firm someday. She's an ungrateful, spoiled brat."

There was a sudden noise, and Nancy looked up to see Lisa standing in the living room doorway. It was clear from her expression that she had heard everything Laurel had said.

Lisa stared at her sister. Then she turned without a word and ran toward the stairs.

"This time I'll catch up with her," Nancy told Ned, starting for the door.

Lisa was in her bedroom, throwing open the bureau drawers. She didn't look up as Nancy entered the room. Nancy hesitated, then sat on the end of her bed.

"Lisa, I'm sorry you heard what Laurel said. I know she hurt your feelings. But you can't blame her, really."

"I don't care how she feels!" Lisa said angrily. "No one ever asks me what *I* want, or how I want to live my life. They just tell me what I'm supposed to do!"

"That *is* hard," Nancy said sympathetically. Whatever trouble Lisa might be causing, at least some of her problems clearly came from the way her father was treating her.

For a moment the guarded look left Lisa's eyes.

When she spoke again, her tone was warmer. "I was rude to you before," she said. "I'm sorry. Things are just a mess lately. And there's no way you could possibly understand what's going on."

"Do you feel like telling me about it, though?" Nancy asked carefully. "Sometimes it helps to talk to someone who isn't part of the family."

Lisa looked down as she spoke. "Well, maybe," she said slowly. "I guess you've gotten sort of a—an impression of my father, right?"

Nancy paused. "He certainly seems to have strong opinions about what you should be doing," she said.

"That's exactly the problem!" Lisa exploded. "I'm nineteen, and he acts like some Victorian father in a book or something! Honestly, I—"

The words poured out in a torrent. Mr. Franklin didn't appreciate Lisa for who she really was. He couldn't imagine that she might want a life of her own. He compared her with Laurel all the time. "Not that I should mind so much," said Lisa with a bitter laugh. "I mean, I usually come out okay in comparison. But—"

And so it went. Nancy was sure that Lisa was finally letting out feelings she'd been holding back for months. But Lisa never said anything about what was specifically bothering her.

After all, Nancy reasoned, probably Mr. Franklin had always been like that. Why was Lisa suddenly so upset now?

And what had been the meaning of that phone call?

As Lisa talked, Nancy noticed that Lisa's mind was wandering. Several times she broke off in midsentence and glanced anxiously around the room. Twice she forgot what she'd been saying and had to start over. Finally Nancy asked, "Is something else the matter?"

Lisa gave a start. "Oh! No, not really. Sorry, Nancy. I—I was just thinking about something I lost. A bracelet."

Nancy saw that the gold bracelet she'd noticed earlier was missing from Lisa's wrist. "Where did you lose it?" she asked.

"Oh, I don't know," said Lisa with a shrug. She sounded as if she were trying to be casual. "I'm sure it's around somewhere." Abruptly she stood up. "It's been nice talking to you, Nancy. Thanks for listening, but I'd like to be alone right now."

"I understand," Nancy said. She left the bedroom and walked quickly down the stairs.

Ned and Laurel were chatting quietly in the living room. "Well? How did it go?" asked Ned as Nancy entered.

"I don't know," said Nancy. "I don't think Lisa really told me anything new. She said I couldn't understand what's going on."

Laurel shook her head. "Lisa may just be making everything into a big deal, the way she always does. She likes attention, if you haven't already figured that out." Laurel yawned. "Time for me to get to bed," she said. "*I* plan to be at the office early tomorrow morning, no matter what Lisa does. I'll just stop in at the library to say good night to my father."

"So Lisa has more or less told me there *is* some kind of mystery, and her sister wants me to think there isn't," Nancy said after Laurel had left the room. "Whom should I believe?"

Ned reached over and squeezed her shoulder. "Why don't you stop thinking about both of them for now?" he said. "Let's go out, just the two of us. I did promise you some fun while we're here in San Francisco."

"You're right," Nancy said. "I'd love to go out. Besides, it's your vacation. You should have some fun, too."

"Let's go ask Laurel or Uncle Bob if they have any good ideas about a place to go," said Ned. "And we'll have to borrow a car."

When Nancy and Ned walked into the library,

Laurel, her father, and Mr. Toomey were going over building plans together. Laurel wasn't going to get to bed right away after all, Nancy thought.

"Hello, kids," said Mr. Franklin, straightening up. "What can I do for you?"

"Well, we were wondering if you could suggest—" Ned began.

Suddenly the phone rang. Mr. Franklin picked it up immediately.

As he listened, his face turned ash white. He gasped, dropped the phone, and leaned back in his chair.

Mr. Toomey leapt up and grabbed the dangling telephone receiver. He listened briefly, then hung up the phone.

"What is it?" Laurel asked.

There was a look of horror on Robert Franklin's face. "That was my night watchman," he said weakly. "Franklin Place is burning down!"

4

A Likely Suspect

"Oh, no!" gasped Laurel. "Dad, what will we do?"

Mr. Franklin clenched his fists. "I've got to get hold of myself," he said through gritted teeth. Then, with a burst of energy, he jumped to his feet. "Christopher, let's get over there," he said.

"Right away, Mr. Franklin," answered Mr. Toomey. His thin face was creased with concern as he and his boss ran from the room.

Laurel raced after them. "Wait, I'm coming too!"

Ned grabbed Nancy's hand. "I'll get Lisa," he said. "Maybe we can follow in her car." He ran to the stairs and called, "Lisa! Lisa, get down here fast!"

Lisa's face appeared at the top of the stairs. "What's going on?" she asked.

When Ned told her, she turned pale. "Oh, no!" she whispered. "It—it can't be!"

"Well, it is," Ned said grimly. "Can you drive us to Franklin Place?"

Lisa was halfway down the stairs. "Let's go!"

But when the three of them arrived, they could see that there had been no point in hurrying.

Franklin Place was totally swallowed by flames that lit the darkness with a nightmarish orange glow. Lisa parked her car next to Mr. Franklin's Lincoln. When she, Nancy, and Ned stepped out of the car, the heat was intense. There was a scorched smell of destruction in the air.

"This is awful," Lisa moaned, standing next to Nancy. In the orange light her face was filled with horror.

A firefighter, his face streaked with black, ran toward them. "Stand back, please!" he ordered.

"Is—is it going to burn to the ground?" Lisa faltered.

"Looks that way," the fireman answered. "We're doing all we can, but the building's too far gone to save much."

Nancy could see that he was right. Everywhere she looked, firefighters were aiming powerful hoses at the flames, but the blaze crackled on. The building's walls were sheets of flame, its steel girders red-hot, and huge sections were crumbling. There was no way to save Franklin Place.

Then Nancy spotted Mr. Franklin. He was standing stock-still as he watched his beloved project disappear before his eyes. Laurel was right beside him, sobbing. Mr. Franklin patted Laurel's shoulder absently, but he continued staring straight ahead.

Mr. Toomey walked up to Nancy, Ned, and Lisa. He looked stunned and sickened. "This is a terrible thing," he said gravely. "All those months of work, all that money spent—if only there were something I could do." He gave a short, humorless laugh. "But the firefighters have made it pretty clear I'd only be in the way."

"You would be." Lisa's voice was harsh. "There's nothing any of us can do."

"Lisa, you don't have to be so rude!" Mr. Toomey protested. "I mean, we're all under a lot of stress, but—"

"*Stress?* Franklin Place is burning down, and you're talking about *stress?*" Lisa shouted. Then she swallowed hard. "I can't take any more of this," she said, trying visibly to control herself. "I'm going to wait by the car for a while."

"I'll keep you company," Ned offered, and Lisa nodded silently. Ned turned to Nancy. "Will you be okay if I—"

"Go ahead," Nancy told him. "I want to look

around a little anyway." She looked at Mr. Toomey. "Please excuse me," she said.

Not that there was anything she expected to turn up. But her investigations had taught Nancy to keep her eyes open whenever anything out of the ordinary happened.

Besides, if she wanted to investigate the building site, now was the time. Nancy knew she had to work quickly. Even after the flames had been extinguished, the firefighters would still be working for hours to make sure the fire didn't flare up again. Ashes could smolder below the ground for days after a fire. The site would be carefully watched. Outsiders would not be welcome. She had to take advantage of the confusion now to make her investigation.

Nancy felt sweat pour down her face. The heat in the air was terrible. Even the ground was roasting. It was so hot that Nancy could feel it through her shoes. The noise of the fire was terrible, too. There was a crackling of the blaze itself, the hiss of steam, the firefighters' hoarse shouts, and in the distance, the wails of more engines rushing to the scene.

Keeping carefully behind the firefighters, Nancy circled the entire building site. She passed a trailer parked behind the site and wondered absently whether it might catch fire, too.

Nancy moved quickly but kept her eyes down,

scanning as much of the ground as she could. It seemed hopeless. She kept stumbling over piles of smoking rubble, and there were many places she couldn't get close to because of the danger. Finally, she made her way back to the front of the building.

There she saw Mr. Toomey and Mr. Franklin standing near the fire trucks. Behind them was a group of reporters. They were all listening to a husky man wearing firefighters' protective clothing and a large badge. He must be the fire chief, Nancy thought.

Suddenly the chief spotted her. "Hey, get away from that building!" he shouted, waving his arms frantically. "What do you think you're doing? Come over here!"

Nancy took one more glance around before hurrying toward him. "Who do you think you are, prowling so close?" the chief yelled.

Mr. Franklin stepped forward. "This is Nancy Drew. She's a guest at my house."

"I'm sorry, Chief," Nancy said. "But I was being very careful. I'm a—"

The chief interrupted her. "Civilians don't belong around dangerous fires," he scolded.

"I'm not exactly a civilian," Nancy began again. "I'm a private investigator, and—"

Again the chief cut her off. "Ms. Drew, we're very busy," he said. "We have a fire to fight. We don't have time to play detective. Why don't you just let us do our jobs?"

"He's right, Nancy," said Mr. Franklin. "Why don't you and Ned go home with Lisa and wait for me there?"

"Fine," Nancy said. But just as she turned to leave, a faint gleam on the ground caught her eye. She reached down to the dirt, and her fingers tangled in a piece of string. She lifted the string, and a hard, bright object came up with it.

Nancy gave a cry of astonishment. The object was Lisa's bracelet!

"What have you got there?" the fire chief asked.

Nancy held up the bracelet with the string tangled around it. "This," she said.

She looked quickly at Mr. Franklin. He didn't seem very interested.

Should I tell him and the chief that it's Lisa's? Nancy wondered. Somehow it seemed wrong to give the chief that information while Mr. Franklin was standing right there. If Mr. Franklin really didn't recognize the bracelet, wouldn't it be better to warn him in private that it belonged to his daughter? Nancy couldn't just surprise him with a fact like that in public—especially when she still wasn't sure whether finding the bracelet here was significant at all.

Nancy handed the fire chief the bracelet. He

stared at it for a moment, turning it over in his hand. "Do you think that could have something to do with the fire?" Nancy asked him carefully.

He shrugged. "Could be, but there's always a lot of junk around a construction site." He handed the bracelet back to Nancy. "Why don't you hang on to this? If I decide it's important, I'll give you a call."

"Any clues as to how the fire started, Chief?" a reporter called out.

As the chief began to speak, Nancy walked to the back of the crowd of reporters. She listened for a few minutes, then hurried back to Lisa's car. Ned and Lisa were waiting for her.

"Hi, Nan!" Ned said as Nancy came up. "Did you find anything?"

Nancy nodded grimly. "I did." She leaned against the car and took a deep breath.

"Lisa, I have something to say," she began, "and you'd better listen closely. The fire chief is talking about arson," Nancy went on. "In fact, he's almost certain someone set the fire on purpose."

"*What?*" Lisa gasped. "You mean it wasn't an accident?"

"That's right." Nancy watched Lisa closely. The girl seemed genuinely surprised.

"But why would someone do that?" Ned asked, puzzled.

"No one knows yet," Nancy replied. "First they

have to investigate to see if it really was arson. Then the police will be brought in. They'll be the ones to hunt for a motive."

"You mean, a motive for destroying Franklin Place?" Ned frowned. "The owner of the building could collect fire insurance," he said. "That would make Uncle Bob a prime suspect, wouldn't it?"

"It might," Nancy said. She glanced at Lisa, who was biting her lip and staring straight ahead. "But if arson was established, and your uncle turned out to be responsible, he wouldn't collect a penny. Besides, I don't think Mr. Franklin would destroy his own work. He was so proud of it. And he certainly doesn't seem to need the insurance money."

"Then who do you think it was, Nan?" asked Ned.

Nancy looked straight at Lisa. "I hate to say this, but right now I have only one suspect. You, Lisa."

"Lisa!" Ned turned and stared at his cousin in shock.

Lisa's eyes were wide with fright. "I was afraid of this," she said in a strangled whisper.

Nancy eyed her thoughtfully. "I know." She reached into the pocket of her brown slacks and drew out Lisa's bracelet.

Lisa gasped. "You found it!"

"I certainly did," said Nancy. "It was right in front of the burning building. Lisa, I saw you with this bracelet before the fire started. You left the house for a short time and then came back—without the bracelet. You do realize that this bracelet is evidence, don't you? It places you right here at the site about the time the fire must have been set."

"I do realize that," said Lisa softly. "Do you have to turn the bracelet over to the fire department?"

Nancy smiled faintly. "Not right now," she answered. "I did tell the chief the truth—that I had found a bracelet. He didn't seem to think it was important, but he might change his mind later."

Lisa lifted her chin. "Finding my bracelet here isn't real evidence that I started the fire."

"That's true." Nancy nodded. "But there are other things to consider."

"Such as?" asked Lisa defiantly.

"Twice tonight you made threats," said Nancy. "First you said you wished Franklin Place would burn down. And the second time, on the telephone, you were talking about making someone sorry."

"You heard that?" Lisa sounded dazed.

Nancy was about to answer when she saw Mr. Franklin striding toward his car. A short, bald man with glasses was hurrying to keep up with him. He

45

looked as if he were trying to talk to Mr. Franklin, but Mr. Franklin wasn't listening. Laurel and Mr. Toomey were right behind them, followed by a crowd of reporters.

When Mr. Franklin reached the car, he paused. "No comment," Nancy heard him say loudly as he opened the door.

A woman reporter stepped out of the crowd. "Is it true that the fire department suspects arson?" she called.

"No comment," Mr. Franklin repeated.

The reporter turned to the short, bald man. "You're Ed Kline, the night watchman, aren't you?" she asked.

The man nodded.

"Did you see anything or anyone suspicious around the building earlier?" the reporter asked.

"Well, yes, as a matter of fact I——"

"He didn't see a thing," Mr. Franklin interrupted. "Good night, Ed. Come on, Laurel, Christopher. Get in."

Suddenly, Ed Kline's jaw dropped. Nancy frowned. He was looking straight at them. "That car!" he exclaimed. "I saw it here earlier tonight! A red Camaro—I'm sure it's the same one."

The night watchman peered more closely at the car. Then his gaze fell on Lisa.

46

"I saw *her*, too! She was here, near the office trailer. Right where the fire broke out. I called to her, and she started running. She took off in this car."

He raised his arm and pointed at Lisa.

"I'm sure of it. *She's* the one who set the fire!"

5

A Wild Ride

"Wait a minute!" shouted Mr. Franklin, turning to the night watchman. "Are you accusing my daughter of—"

Ed Kline set his jaw. "I certainly am," he said flatly. He jerked his head toward Lisa. "She's the one who set the fire," he repeated.

There was a shocked silence. Then everyone started talking at once. Reporters swarmed around Lisa's car, yelling questions. Electronic flashes began exploding in the dark. Lisa hid her face against the side of the car. Ned and Nancy stepped in front of her.

Mr. Franklin held up his hand in the manner of a man who was used to being obeyed. "Please, everyone, it's been a rough night," he called.

The reporters paid no attention. They pressed in

even closer, scribbling frantically and firing questions.

"Mr. Franklin, did you have any suspicions that your daughter was going to set this fire?"

"Does she have a criminal record?"

"Did you know it was arson, sir?"

Mr. Franklin threw both hands into the air. "I have no comment! No more questions!" he shouted angrily. "You're all jumping to conclusions. No one has confirmed arson! Save your questions for the fire chief."

He turned back toward his car once again, but a reporter blocked his way.

"Sir, why would your daughter set fire to your own building?" she asked. "Is there a problem—"

Mr. Franklin's expression turned ugly. He elbowed the reporter out of the way so roughly that she stumbled backward. "I told you, I won't answer any questions," he growled. "Speak to the chief, why don't you?"

"And here comes the chief now," Nancy said under her breath. "Maybe that will distract them for a while."

As the crowd of reporters turned toward the fire chief, Nancy opened Lisa's car door. "This looks like a good time for us to leave," she told Lisa. "Ned or I will drive if you'd like."

Lisa nodded shakily. She climbed into the back of the car and slumped against the seat.

Laurel had edged over to Nancy. She still had a shocked look on her face. "Nancy, could Lisa really have done it?" she asked.

"We'll need lots more evidence before we can be sure who did it," Nancy said.

To her surprise, Laurel seemed angry. "That's right—protect Lisa!" she burst out. "Everyone always has to take care of Lisa, even when she's committed a crime!" She turned her back on Nancy and headed toward her father's car.

What did *that* mean? Nancy wondered. Laurel sounded as if she wanted her to think Lisa set the fire. Why would Laurel want anyone to think that? Unless . . .

Nancy shook her head. This case was only a few hours old, but it was growing more complicated by the minute.

As she was climbing into the front seat Nancy heard the fire chief tell Mr. Franklin, "I'll talk with you later, sir." She paused for a moment to listen.

"It looks bad," the chief was saying. "Where can I reach you if there's any news?"

"Call me at home or the office anytime," answered Mr. Franklin.

He turned to Ned. "I want you to drive Lisa and Nancy," he ordered. "Don't stop to talk to anyone."

"Yes, Uncle Bob," Ned answered.

Mr. Franklin motioned to Laurel and Mr. Toomey to get into the Lincoln.

Ned got into the driver's seat of Lisa's car, and Nancy settled in on the passenger side. As Ned pulled the car into the road, Nancy turned to face Lisa.

"Those reporters are going to ask even more questions tomorrow, you know. Your father won't be able to keep them away forever. It might help if we talked things over first."

Lisa dropped her head into her hands. "What for? It's hopeless!"

"Maybe not," Nancy said. "Just tell us the truth."

Lisa shook her head. "I can't," she choked out.

Ned glanced at his cousin in the rearview mirror and frowned. Then he looked at Nancy. "Lisa's no criminal. She's not guilty, Nancy. I won't believe that."

Lisa gave him a grateful look. "Thanks," she murmured.

"It's too early to tell who's really guilty," Nancy said. "But the only evidence right now points to you."

"I just can't say anything" was Lisa's reply. "I'm sorry."

"Please, Lisa," Ned urged. "You'll feel better if you stop hiding whatever it is you're hiding."

Lisa shook her head.

"We'll have to tell the police about this eventually, you know," Nancy said gently. "Finding your bracelet at the site, those threats you made—it doesn't look good for you, Lisa. And putting that evidence together with the fact that the night watchman saw you around the time the fire was set . . ." Her voice trailed away.

Terror mingled with stubbornness on Lisa's face. "They can't prove I set the fire," she said. "They can't prove I had a reason to set it, either." She clamped her jaw shut and stared out the window.

"Your family will think you had a reason," Ned pointed out.

Nancy decided to try a different tack. "Lisa," she said, "if you didn't set the fire, what were you doing at the site?"

"I'm sorry," Lisa answered. "I can't tell you that, either."

They drove the rest of the way home in silence.

Mr. Franklin, Mr. Toomey, and Laurel were waiting for them in the living room when they arrived. For a moment no one said anything. Then Mr. Franklin cleared his throat.

"I just talked to the fire chief," he said. "Larson, his name is. They found an incendiary device at the site. It was definitely arson."

Lisa collapsed into a chair.

"Chief Larson has already called the police," said Mr. Franklin tiredly. "There'll be a scandal, I'm afraid. Lisa, if you did this, why? How could you betray me this way?"

Lisa stared down at her hands.

"Well, Lisa?" asked Laurel bitingly. "Don't you have anything to say?"

Lisa looked up. "I'm really sorry," she quavered. "But you all have to believe me. I had nothing to do with setting the fire. I could never do such a terrible thing."

Mr. Franklin's gaze softened for a moment. Then he drew himself up. "Nancy, can you help clear Lisa's name?" he asked.

"I certainly hope so," said Nancy. She wanted to believe Lisa was innocent, too. But she couldn't ignore the fact that Lisa was obviously holding something back. Until she could prove otherwise, Lisa was the prime suspect right now.

"The first thing we need to do is go over alibis," Nancy said. "We were all here at the time of the fire. The only one who left the house was Lisa."

"I told you, I didn't set the fire!" Lisa insisted.

"Then maybe you saw someone who did," Nancy said. "Think, Lisa, did you notice anything strange? A car? Signs of another person?"

Lisa shook her head helplessly. "No."

53

Mr. Franklin sighed. "But why did you want to hide the fact that you were at Franklin Place?"

Lisa jumped up. "I'm not trying to hide anything!" she burst out. "I knew you'd all think I was guilty! You never believe anything I say!"

"Wait a minute," said Nancy. "All of this has been a shock, I know. But getting mad at one another won't help."

"Nancy's right," said Ned. Lisa sat down again.

Laurel leaned forward in her chair. "There *is* one other possibility," she said hesitantly, glancing at her sister. "Richard Bates, Lisa's boyfriend."

"No, no! Not Richard!" Lisa cried. "Why would he destroy Franklin Place?"

"He might have done it to—well, to help you," Laurel answered. "Richard did drive you home today after you called from the office and asked him to pick you up. And you know what kind of a mood you were in then."

"What does that have to do with arson?" Lisa snapped.

Laurel bit her lip. "Well, did you tell Richard you wished Franklin Place would burn to the ground? I'm only trying to help," she added quickly.

Lisa looked frightened again. "I may have said something like that," she admitted. "But Richard's the *last* person who would set a fire. You have to believe me. He'd never do anything like that!"

54

Mr. Franklin seemed to have run out of patience. "Well, Lisa, according to you, no one set the fire."

"I didn't say that!" cried Lisa hotly.

"Calm down, everyone," Nancy said. "Lisa, this may be important. Where was Richard this evening after he dropped you at home?"

"I don't know, but he wasn't with me," Lisa answered.

"You're sure you didn't ask him to meet you at Franklin Place?"

"No," Lisa insisted. "He dropped me off here, and he left. I don't know where he went after that."

Mr. Franklin squared his shoulders decisively. There was a look of relief on his face. "Well, Nancy," he said briskly, "I think it's pretty clear that your first job is to investigate Richard Bates. I suggest you do it right away."

"No!" Lisa shouted.

Nancy and Ned exchanged looks. "Your father is right," Nancy told Lisa. "And if you don't mind, I'd like to use your car to drive to San Rafael tomorrow morning."

Lisa thought for a moment. "Okay," she answered finally. "But only if I go along."

"No way," Nancy said quickly. "It's best if you stay home tomorrow. The police and fire chief may want to ask you questions. If you're not here, it could look suspicious."

"Oh, all right," Lisa grumbled. Abruptly, she stood up. "I'm exhausted," she said with a huge yawn. "I'm going to bed right now."

Nancy was surprised when both Mr. Franklin and Laurel smiled. "Family joke," Laurel explained. "Lisa falls asleep at the drop of a hat—and once she's asleep, there's no way to wake her up. If she doesn't go up now, we'll have to drag her upstairs."

"I think we should *all* go to bed," Mr. Franklin announced. "Tomorrow's going to be a rough day, I'm afraid. Christopher, can you show yourself out?"

Mr. Toomey had been so quiet until now that Nancy had almost forgotten he was there. Now he stood up quickly. "Of course," he said. "Unless there's anything more I can do for you tonight, sir."

"No, no," said Mr. Franklin with a smile. "You've been helpful enough already. You go home and get some rest."

"All right," Mr. Toomey said. "Good night, everyone."

Although she'd said she was sleepy, Lisa wasn't in the bedroom when Nancy went upstairs. Nancy stepped back into the hall and saw that the telephone cord was stretched away from the table again.

She stepped quietly toward the alcove. Lisa was curled up inside, speaking in a hushed, urgent voice. Nancy couldn't catch anything she was saying.

Just then a window slammed down somewhere in the house. Startled, Lisa looked up and saw Nancy watching her. She slammed down the receiver and scrambled to her feet.

"I—uh—was just calling a friend about some homework," she said.

Nancy said nothing. Had Lisa called Richard to warn him?

As if she had read Nancy's mind, Lisa rushed up and grabbed her by the shoulders. "Nancy, Richard is the sweetest, nicest boy in the world," she declared. "He couldn't do anything wrong. Not Richard!"

"That's probably what we'll find out, then," said Nancy reassuringly. "Don't worry, Lisa. And don't do anything foolish. Promise?"

"Sure," Lisa muttered.

It had been a long day. Nancy fell asleep quickly, but she didn't sleep very soundly. Strange dreams kept flickering around the edges of her mind.

She was lying in a dark, square room. Doors kept opening and shutting, but for some reason Nancy couldn't open her eyes. A shadowy figure stared down at her, then flitted silently away. What did it want?

Nancy sat bolt upright. Lisa was sleeping peacefully in the bed across the room. The only sound outside was the chirping of birds.

Just a dream, Nancy told herself with relief, and fell back to sleep.

When she woke up again, sun was streaming into the room. Lisa was still asleep. Nancy washed and dressed as quietly as she could, then slipped out of the room and went downstairs.

Ned was waiting for her in the breakfast room. "Looks as though we're about the last ones up," he said. "Mr. Toomey came and picked up Laurel and Uncle Bob about a half hour ago. They're on their way to talk to the fire chief. They left us a road map showing how to get to San Rafael."

"Then let's go," said Nancy. Quickly, she drained a glass of juice and picked up a blueberry muffin from the basket on the table. "It's a gorgeous day," she said. "At least we'll have a nice drive."

The road to San Rafael curved through deep green woods filled with giant redwood trees. Then it climbed high into the mountains, giving breathtaking views of the valleys below.

Nancy was enjoying herself at the wheel. Lisa's red Camaro handled easily, and a fresh, crisp breeze was blowing through the open windows. "Wow!" she said. "Look at that!" On one side of the road the land dropped sharply in a steep, jagged

58

cliff. "We sure don't have hills like this in River Heights!"

"I'll watch the view. *You* watch the road," said Ned.

"Oh, don't worry. I'm paying attention," said Nancy. They were heading across a patch of rough gravel into a tight curve now. Nancy swung the wheel to take the curve.

To her surprise, the car didn't respond. It seemed to drag slightly, as though she'd stepped on the brakes. Then it swerved to the left.

"What's going on?" Nancy said. She slowed down as they rounded the curve, then stepped lightly on the gas.

All of a sudden everything went wrong.

The car lurched horribly, then swerved onto the shoulder. Nancy slammed her foot down on the brakes. The rear end of the Camaro skidded into the guardrail on the opposite side. "We're out of control!" she cried, trying frantically to steer the car back into the lane.

Then the car swung wildly around. The last thing Nancy saw was the sheer drop off the edge of the road.

6

All in Black

There was a terrible thud, and Nancy was hurled against the steering wheel. The car slammed against the guardrail and jumped forward again. It spun, nearly flipping over. For a terrifying moment Nancy was afraid they were going to pitch over the cliff. Then the Camaro hit the guardrail at an angle and shuddered to a stop.

Nancy had closed her eyes while the car was spinning. Now she opened them and looked out the window.

All she could see was the sheer drop down a ravine filled with jagged rocks and rubble.

A wave of faintness washed over Nancy. She leaned against the steering wheel and forced herself to breathe deeply.

"Are you all right?" asked Ned. He was very pale, but otherwise he looked unhurt.

"I'm fine." Nancy reached over and squeezed his hand. "How are you?" she asked.

"No broken bones," Ned said with a smile. "I never doubted your driving for a minute." Still, Nancy could see that he was shaken by their close call.

"We'd better check the damage," Nancy said. "I guess I'll have to get out on your side." The left side of the car was wedged tightly against the guardrail.

A quick look revealed that the left side of the car was badly dented. They had also bent the guardrail. Nancy was grateful the low fence had done its job.

"We sure were lucky," Ned said, echoing her thoughts. Together they peered down the side of the steep ravine.

Nancy shuddered. If it hadn't been for the guardrail, they could easily have been killed.

Ned walked around to the back of the car. "The left tire is flat," he called. "That must be what put us into the skid."

Nancy hurried to Ned's side. They would have to change the tire, but first they'd have to get the car away from the rail. She got behind the wheel to steer while Ned pushed the car toward the road. They moved it very slowly, inching it away from the rail. When it was safely on the shoulder, Nancy set the brake.

After she and Ned had changed the flat tire, they lowered the Camaro back down. Ned inspected the damaged tire and gave a long, low whistle. "Take a look at that!" he said.

Nancy knelt beside him. Ned tilted the tire, pointing to a spot where a neat hole had burst through.

"That explains it," Ned said, shaking his head. "We really had a close call. A blowout like that is super dangerous."

"Only I don't think it was a blowout," Nancy said slowly. "In fact, I don't think it was an accident at all."

Nancy pointed to the puncture. It was a clean, round hole. "This hole was made with some kind of sharp instrument," she said. "And there was no loud explosion the way there would be with a blowout."

Nancy stood up and brushed the dirt off the knees of her jeans. "This was no accident, Ned. Someone punctured that tire on purpose."

Ned looked stunned. "You're right. There was no explosion, now that I think of it. But who would do something like this? And why?"

Nancy scanned the road in both directions. "My guess is that the tire was punctured before we left the house. We were supposed to have a flat tire and lose air slowly while we drove along. By the time the tire was completely flat, we'd be stranded."

"What are you saying?" Ned asked.

"That someone wanted to keep us from reaching San Rafael University right away."

Ned raised his brows. "Lisa?"

Nancy nodded. Quickly, she told Ned about seeing Lisa talking on the phone the night before. "She said she was calling a friend about homework, but I didn't believe her," Nancy said. Then she described the strange dream she'd had. "Now I think I wasn't dreaming," Nancy said. "I think I must have woken up enough to sense Lisa coming and going from the bedroom."

"But Laurel said Lisa was a sound sleeper," Ned reminded her.

"Maybe she was pretending to be asleep," Nancy said. "I think she was worried that warning Richard wouldn't be enough. She wanted to make sure we wouldn't talk to him. So she got up in the middle of the night, sneaked out to the garage, and poked a hole in the tire of her car. I'm sure she didn't realize that these sharp curves and gravel would make our flat tire much more serious."

"What a crazy thing for her to do," Ned said angrily. "She put our lives in danger!"

"I'm sure she didn't think of it that way," Nancy

63

pointed out. "Lisa was just trying to protect Richard." Nancy frowned. "I wonder if she thinks he's guilty of setting the fire.

"Anyway, her plan worked. So far, at least," Nancy continued. "We've definitely lost a lot of time. Chances are, we won't be able to find Richard anyway. Lisa's already warned him about us."

Ned grabbed Nancy's hand and pulled her toward the car. "So what are we waiting for?" he said. "Let's get moving."

San Rafael University was set on a huge, rolling campus. As Nancy and Ned drove up to a visitors' parking lot, they noticed a small building with a sign that read Information.

Inside the building a slender young man of about twenty-five was sitting at a desk.

"Hi," he said in a friendly voice. "Can I help you?"

"I hope so." Nancy smiled. "Do you have a student directory we can use? We're looking for someone named Richard Bates."

"Sure thing. Lots of students are away, though. It's semester break."

"We're pretty sure Richard's still here," Nancy said.

The young man pulled a thick book out of one of

his desk drawers and began flipping through the pages. "Bates. A senior, right?" he asked.

"He lives off campus," said Nancy. "Do you have his address?"

"I'm sorry, but we don't list off-campus addresses," the young man told her. "His phone's unlisted, too."

Nancy sighed. "Well, thanks, anyway." Then she turned to Ned. "I feel as though we're on a wild goose chase," she said.

Ned grinned. "Don't give up yet. If this place is anything like Emerson, we should have some luck." Emerson was Ned's college.

"Can you tell us where to find the student union?" he asked the guard.

"Sure." The young man gave them directions. "It's about a five-minute walk," he said.

The campus was a lovely setting, with rolling green lawns and a view of the mountains in the distance. Most of the old brick buildings were shaded by big trees.

"This is beautiful," Nancy said as they walked. "I'm really starting to fall in love with California. Don't worry, though," she added teasingly. "I'll be sure to visit River Heights once in a while."

The student union was a sprawling modern building. It had been built around an open courtyard that was filled with round patio tables. Colorful striped umbrellas shielded the tables from the sun. Nancy could tell that the courtyard was a popular spot on campus. Even during vacation it was filled with students coming and going. The air was buzzing with conversation.

Nancy and Ned headed toward a table where three students—two girls and a boy—were sitting.

"Mind if we sit here?" Nancy asked. She nodded at the two empty seats next to one of the girls, who had long blond hair and a friendly smile.

"Not at all," the blond girl answered. She pushed her things aside to make room for them.

"We're from out of town," Nancy said as she and Ned sat down. "I was thinking of going to school here. Actually, we came here so I could look someone up and talk to him about it."

"Who is he?" the blond girl asked with interest.

"He's a senior named Richard Bates. Do you know him?"

All three students shook their heads. "We're just freshmen, though," said the blond girl. "We don't know that many upperclassmen. Let's ask someone else."

She craned her neck, looking around, then waved at a boy and girl across the courtyard who looked a couple of years older. "That's my dorm counselor,

66

Sue Evans, and her boyfriend," she told Nancy. "They might know your friend."

When the couple approached their table, the blond girl quickly explained that Nancy and Ned were visiting the campus. "They're looking for a senior named Richard Bates," she said. "Do either of you know him?"

Sue Evans, a perky-looking brunette, nodded. "Isn't he the guy who goes out with Lisa Franklin?"

"We know Lisa," Nancy explained. "Lisa was the one who suggested that I talk to Richard."

Sue nodded. "Well, he's kind of shy. Except for going around with Lisa, he keeps pretty much to himself. I think he lives off campus, too. But I'll tell you where you might find him. Try Perry Hall. That's the architecture building. Richard hangs out there a lot, even on vacations." Quickly she gave them directions to Perry Hall.

"Thanks so much," said Nancy as she and Ned got up to leave. "Oh! By the way, how will I recognize Richard? I've never seen him before."

Sue laughed. "That's easy. He's medium height, on the stocky side. He has brown hair and brown eyes."

Ned laughed. "Sounds like a lot of guys."

"Yes, but there is one thing different about Richard. He wears all black. All the time."

"Hey, wait a minute!" Sue's boyfriend said suddenly. "Isn't that Richard over there?"

He pointed across the courtyard. Nancy saw a boy dressed in a black turtleneck and black jeans. He was walking toward the tables, balancing a stack of books and a tray.

Before Nancy could say anything, Sue's boyfriend had called, "Hey, Bates! Here's someone looking for you!" He pointed at Nancy.

Richard Bates froze in his tracks. Suddenly he hurled his tray aside and dashed out of the courtyard.

"Wait!" Nancy called. "I have to talk to you!"

But Richard Bates was already out of sight.

7

Danger at the Tower

"We've got to stop him!" Nancy shouted.

Ned and Nancy raced out of the courtyard after Richard Bates. "Hey! Clean up those fries!" Nancy heard someone calling after them. But the most important thing to think about now was catching Richard.

Unfortunately, there was no sign of him anywhere. A few curious students stared at Nancy and Ned as they slowed, panting, to a stop. But the boy in black seemed to have vanished completely.

"We've lost him," said Ned in disgust.

Nancy sighed. "Lisa must have told him what we look like."

"Well, what now?" Ned asked.

"I'm not sure," said Nancy with a frown. "Let's try Perry Hall anyway. Maybe we'll find out something so this trip won't be a total loss."

After asking directions, Nancy and Ned located the architecture building. It was made of poured concrete with irregularly placed windows and a row of skylights in the roof. Nancy tried the main door; it was unlocked. She and Ned stepped inside and found themselves in a long tiled hall.

"Looks deserted," said Ned.

They walked down the hall, peeking into empty lecture rooms and studios through the windows in their locked doors. The tables in the studios were covered with blueprints and sketches.

At the end of the hall Nancy turned to face Ned. "I guess this is a bust," she said disappointedly. "There's no one here who—"

Suddenly she heard a door behind her opening. "Who are you? What are you doing here?" someone asked fiercely.

Nancy whirled around. A dark-haired man stood in a studio doorway, glaring at her and Ned. He was in his fifties and had glasses pushed up onto his forehead. His shirt-sleeves were rolled up, and his hands looked grimy, as if he had been drawing with charcoal.

"We're looking for someone," she told the man. "His name is Richard Bates. Do you know him, by any chance?"

Instantly, the man's glare was replaced by a look of surprise. His eyes lit up behind his glasses.

"Bates! Why, he's my prize pupil!" he exclaimed. "You're in luck. He should be back any minute. He just stepped out to grab a bite to eat."

Somehow Nancy doubted Richard would return to Perry Hall now.

The man stepped forward and held out his hand. "I'm Ed Strong," he said. "Professor of architecture. Any friend of Bates's is a friend of mine. He's a dedicated boy, you know, with a very promising future."

As Nancy introduced herself and Ned, she found herself thinking that Richard's future wouldn't be too promising if he had anything to do with the arson at Franklin Place. She didn't even know for sure if Richard was a suspect, she reminded herself.

"Come on into my studio and wait for him, if you like," Professor Strong invited them.

"Thank you," Nancy replied with a smile. "That would be great."

Professor Strong's studio was filled with large worktables. The one closest to the door was completely covered with a cardboard model. It looked to Nancy like a village of the future—a series of small houses linked by overhead walkways. In the center was a large structure that looked like some kind of recreation area.

"This is a nice model," she commented, touching one of the cardboard buildings gently. "I like the way it would give people privacy and a sense of community at the same time."

Professor Strong smiled approvingly. "It's an exciting project, isn't it?" he asked. "Bates and Franklin did this. Really promising students, both of them."

"Lisa Franklin?" Nancy asked. "I didn't know she and Richard were doing a project together."

The professor nodded. "They're doing some of the best work I've seen in a long time," he said. "Lisa's ideas are brilliant. It's really too bad—" He broke off.

"What's too bad?" Nancy asked.

"Talent going to waste," the professor answered with a shrug. "Lisa will never actually get to build anything like this. Her father likes tamer stuff, and she'll be working for him." He shook his head sadly.

The image of Lisa's bedroom floated into Nancy's mind. Lisa's carefully impersonal bedroom, where there wasn't a single touch of character—nothing as original as the cardboard model in this studio.

Lisa must hide this side of her life from her father, Nancy thought. Maybe she knows he'd disapprove, so she doesn't even let him see her designs. Over time, that kind of concealment would build up into a lot of pressure.

But was it enough pressure to make someone commit arson?

Nancy realized that Professor Strong and Ned were eyeing her curiously. "Speaking of Lisa Franklin," she said, "have you heard about what happened to Franklin Place?"

"I certainly have. I read about it in this morning's paper. The police suspect arson, as I recall." He sighed. "It would be a shame if any scandal came near Lisa. As I said, she's a talented girl."

"Professor Strong," Nancy said, "I have a question that could be very important. Do you know where Richard Bates was last night?"

The professor hesitated. "Well, now," he said slowly. "I don't see why I should tell you anything."

"Now, look—" Ned burst out indignantly. But Nancy laid a hand on his arm. "It's okay, Ned," she said. "He has a right to ask." She turned back to Professor Strong.

"I'm a private detective. And Ned is Lisa's cousin," she explained. "The two of us are here to try to help Lisa—and Richard. Unfortunately, some people think Lisa may have had something to do with the fire at Franklin Place. A few people also suspect Richard."

After a moment Professor Strong nodded slowly. "I guess it wouldn't do any harm to answer your question," he said. "Well, Richard was here yesterday, working on this project. I do know he got one phone call sometime after four o'clock."

"That's about when Lisa would have called him to pick her up at the office," Nancy said thoughtfully.

The professor shrugged. "I don't know who it was. But after the call, Richard left the studio for a couple of hours. He came back around six-thirty."

So there were two hours not entirely accounted for, Nancy thought. That was plenty of time to set a fire and get back to San Rafael before the blaze really got going.

"Richard came back and put in three more hours of work," the professor went on. "And he was just as calm and collected as before he left. There's no way I'd believe he was out causing trouble."

"No one's trying to pin any blame on Richard," said Nancy quietly. "But I guess we've taken up enough of your time. We won't wait around for him any longer. Thank you very much, Professor Strong."

She was aware of the man's doubtful stare as she and Ned left the studio.

"It looks even worse for Lisa and Richard now," Ned said grimly as they walked out of Perry Hall.

"I'm afraid so," said Nancy. "Believe me, Ned, I *want* to prove that your cousin is innocent. But at

74

this point I can't promise that's what's going to happen."

She checked her watch quickly. "You know, I think we should find a pay phone and call the Franklins," she said. "They may be wondering what's keeping us."

There was a telephone a few feet down the path from the architecture building. When Nancy dialed the Franklins' number, Laurel picked up on the first ring.

"Nancy!" she said in surprise. "Did you make it to San Rafael okay?"

Now, why would she ask me that? Nancy wondered. "Yes, we're fine," she said carefully. "It took us a little longer to get here than we expected, though. What's happening at the house?"

"Oh, Nancy!" Laurel wailed. "The police just left—and it was awful! They asked us all kinds of questions, and they kept pestering Lisa. It looks bad, Nancy. It really does. I think Lisa's in a lot of trouble."

"What did you tell the police?" Nancy asked.

"Nothing they didn't already know." Nancy thought Laurel sounded a little defensive. "The night watchman had already told them he thought Lisa had done it. And they asked us whether Lisa had ever made any kind of threats." Laurel's voice rose. "We had to tell the truth, didn't we?"

"It's always best to tell the police the truth," Nancy answered calmly. But were Lisa's threats the truth Laurel *wanted* the police to know? she wondered. "Could I speak to Lisa?" she asked.

"I don't think so," Laurel said. Now there was an unmistakable tone of anger in her voice. "After the police left, she went upstairs and locked herself in her room. She wouldn't tell them why she went to the site. She said only that she'd been upset about work, that she took a drive and ended up at Franklin Place. Then, she said, she looked around a bit and came home. The police didn't really go for that explanation, of course."

Nancy sighed as she hung up the phone. "I hate to say this, Ned, but Laurel sounds like a real goody-goody sometimes. I can see why Lisa doesn't want to tell her anything."

Nancy filled him in on what Laurel had said.

Ned shook his head ruefully. "Sounds bad," he said. Suddenly Ned gave Nancy a quick hug. "Look, Nan. You're exhausted, and so am I," he said. "It's been a rough two days. I say it's time for us to take a break. Let's pretend we're tourists and do some sight-seeing. Okay?"

"That sounds great," said Nancy wistfully. "But don't you think we should get back to the Franklins'? We should at least tell Lisa about what happened to her car."

"She's sulking in her room," Ned pointed out. "Come on, Nancy. You've earned a break."

Nancy smiled. "You're a persuasive guy, Nickerson. Okay, I'll take a break. For the rest of the afternoon let's just have a nice, quiet time together."

The view from Coit Tower was spectacular. Nancy and Ned were high atop Telegraph Hill. It seemed as though all of San Francisco lay at their feet.

"This was really worth it," Nancy said. She gazed out at the view and took Ned's hand. "Let's stop at the gift shop before we climb the tower," she suggested. "I'd like to get some postcards."

The gift shop was on the bottom floor of the tower, and a good-size crowd was already packed inside. "On second thought, maybe we should come back later," said Nancy. "I don't want to spend the whole afternoon waiting in line."

"We can take the elevator," said Ned. An elevator in the gift shop led to the observation room on the top floor.

"No, let's walk," said Nancy. "It's only two hundred and ten feet," she added with a grin.

Ten minutes later they reached the top of the narrow spiral staircase.

It was a perfect, sunny day. The sky overhead was

a clear, crisp blue with tiny wisps of cloud. Far below, the blue was reflected in the harbor, whose surface was dotted with ships.

The top floor was crowded with families and tour groups. Nancy and Ned threaded their way through the people until they reached the edge of the roof. There a number of viewing machines had been set up. Nancy took out some change, slipped the coins into one of the machines, and swung the machine around.

"This is wonderful," she murmured, her eyes glued to the view. "Hey, look, Ned! I think I can see Franklin Place—or what's left of it."

Ned tapped her shoulder. "I thought we agreed. No detective business this afternoon, okay?"

He grabbed the viewer and swung it in the opposite direction.

Laughing, Nancy started to reach for the viewer again. Then she spotted someone across the observation deck from them and gasped.

"Nan, what's wrong?" asked Ned.

"Look!" Nancy said, pointing. "Richard Bates is here!"

Lisa's boyfriend was standing at the edge of the tower, staring toward the distant ruins of Franklin Place.

Nancy took a step forward into the crowd. "Richard!" she called.

He spun around at the sound of his name, terror in his eyes. Then he darted toward the stairway. But just then a group of kids came rushing up the stairs and blocked his way.

That gave Nancy the few seconds she needed to catch up to Richard. She grabbed his arm as he started headlong down the stairs.

"Nancy, watch out!" Ned yelled.

It was too late. Nancy had already lost her balance at the edge of the stairs. In the next instant she was flying through space. The only sound she heard was her own scream of fear.

8

Then There Were Three

For a sickening moment Nancy thought she was going to drop straight to the ground. Then her body hit the stone steps with a thud. She plummeted down them over and over, her arms and legs flailing in all directions. Walls and stairs rushed by in mixed-up flashes.

Finally, she was at the bottom. Nancy lay gasping for breath. She hurt too badly to move.

She was vaguely aware of people running down the stairs toward her, but she couldn't lift her head to look at them. "Are you all right? Are you all right?" dozens of people seemed to be saying as they gathered around her.

All right? Nancy still felt dazed. Her head was pounding, and she had to blink to bring things into focus. Her whole body felt sore, and one hand was throbbing especially painfully.

Now Ned's voice reached her through the crowd. "Nancy!" he called. "I'm almost there!"

In a few seconds he was at her side and holding her hand. Nancy smiled faintly. "Boy, am I glad to see you!" she whispered, struggling to sit up.

"Hang on. Don't move yet," Ned cautioned her. "This woman's going to check you out first."

A kindly-looking elderly woman was right behind Ned. "I'm Margot Liston," she said. "I work in the gift shop. I've had a lot of first-aid training. Please don't move until I've checked to see whether you have any broken bones."

Nancy felt completely alert now. "I don't think anything's broken," she said as the woman finished a gentle examination. "I bet I'll be pretty sore for a few days, though."

"You're a lucky girl," the woman said. "That was a nasty fall. You'll be pretty badly bruised, but there's no serious harm." She turned to Ned. "Can you take her home?"

"I sure can," said Ned. He helped Nancy to her feet. Nancy swayed with dizziness, but Ned tightened his grip around her waist. "How do you feel now?" he asked, his face still pale with concern.

"A little shaky," Nancy admitted. "I really hurt my left hand knocking it against the wall."

"What do you want us to do with this guy, miss?" came a voice in the crowd.

Nancy looked up and saw three angry-looking men holding Richard Bates firmly against the wall. He was pale, too, and looked terrified. "We saw him drag you down the stairs. We caught him before he could get away," one of the men said. "Do you want us to call the police? You've got lots of witnesses here."

Richard Bates made a helpless gesture. "I'm not going to run away," he said.

"Well, that's what you *were* doing!" Ned snapped furiously. "First you pull her down the stairs. Then you run like a coward! I'd like to throw *you* down the—"

"Hold it, Ned," Nancy interrupted weakly. With Ned still supporting her, she hobbled toward Richard Bates.

"I—I was just trying to get away," he faltered. "I wasn't trying to hurt you, honest. You've got to let me explain. I—"

"Believe me, I *want* an explanation," Nancy said grimly. "In fact, if you don't tell me what's going on, I'll turn you over to the police right now."

Bates flinched. "Please don't! I'll—I'll talk to you."

"Fine," Ned put in. "But not here. I've got to get Nancy back to the Franklins'. You can follow us there. And if you don't, we'll find you soon enough."

It was four-thirty in the afternoon. Nancy had just finished a long, hot soak in the tub, and she was feeling much better. She stretched out on the bed with a sigh of relief just as Laurel walked in, carrying a tray of tea and cookies. Behind her were Ned, Lisa, and Richard. Lisa and Richard looked like little kids whose teacher was about to scold them.

Laurel's lips were tight as she set down the tray. "The doctor will be here in about an hour. I'll come back for this tray later on," she said coldly. She shot Richard an angry look and flounced out of the room.

"Ready to talk, Nan?" asked Ned.

"Let me just drink some tea," Nancy answered. She took a few sips, then propped herself up on her pillows.

"You know that Richard didn't mean for anything to happen to you, right?" said Lisa quickly. "He would never do something like—"

"Wait a minute, Lisa," Nancy said. "My first question is for you. You *did* call Richard to warn him last night, didn't you? You wanted him to know that Ned and I were driving up to see him."

"No," Lisa said firmly. "I already told you. I was calling someone else about schoolwork!"

Nancy didn't miss the nervous glance Richard gave Lisa.

"Then why did Richard run as soon as he saw us at the student union?" she asked.

Before Lisa could answer, Richard cut in. "It's no use, Lisa," he said. "Stop trying." He turned to Nancy. "Lisa *did* call me late last night. She told me you'd be coming to San Rafael to question me and that I should stay away from you. Then she hung up really suddenly."

"Probably because I saw her talking on the phone," Nancy said dryly. "But if you had nothing to hide, what did Lisa have to warn you about?"

"The fire, of course," said Richard. "She told me some people might think I had set it. Then I saw the newspaper this morning. The article made it sound as though *Lisa* had set the fire. When you and Ned showed up at school, I thought you might trap me somehow. You know, make me say things that could hurt Lisa. I guess I panicked."

Lisa gave him a half smile. "I panicked, too, Richard. I was afraid you really *had* burned down Franklin Place."

"How could you think that?" Richard sounded genuinely astonished. "Besides, I couldn't possibly

84

have had the chance to do it. I was at the studio all day and night."

"Except for those two hours when you picked Lisa up at the office and drove her home," Nancy put in quietly. "We've already talked to Professor Strong."

A fleeting look of anger crossed Richard's face. "You've been doing your homework, I see," he muttered.

"Well, that's what we're here for," Nancy reminded him. "But we still don't know why you followed us to Coit Tower."

"I was so worried about Lisa," said Richard. He let his hands fall open helplessly. "I was afraid you were trying to prove she'd set the fire. I thought if I kept track of where you went, I could warn *her*—or maybe head you off."

"Head us off?" Ned repeated angrily. "You dragged Nancy headfirst down the stairs when she tried to catch up with you."

Richard winced. "I really didn't mean to hurt her," he protested. "I was going so fast I didn't even notice she was holding my sleeve!"

"He's telling the truth," Lisa put in. "He would never do anything to hurt *anyone*."

"I hope you're both right," said Nancy gravely. "But it's not the only time I was in danger today.

Lisa, didn't you realize that puncturing the tire on your car could have caused a serious accident? Ned and I were lucky not to have gone over the guard-rail."

Lisa looked puzzled. "What are you talking about?" she asked. "I don't know anything about a punctured tire. Wait a minute! I saw a dent in my car when you came in, but I didn't get a chance to ask about it."

"The tire was definitely punctured," said Nancy.

Lisa stared at her in horror. "But you don't think I'd do that to you, do you?" she asked.

Nancy frowned slightly. "Lisa, I want to believe you about everything. But you lied when you said you hadn't called Richard. Now you say you didn't cause our flat tire. How can I be sure you're telling the truth this time?"

"Oh, this is so frustrating!" cried Lisa. "Because this time I *am* telling the truth, that's all! And if you don't believe me—"

She broke off with a mirthless laugh. "Well, if you don't believe me, I guess that's my own fault, isn't it?"

"Ned said you wanted to talk to me," Laurel said about a half hour later.

Nancy looked up from her pillows. "That's right,

I did. Thanks for the tea, first of all. It really hit the spot."

"Oh, you're welcome." Laurel was standing awkwardly in the doorway. "What did Lisa and Richard tell you?" she asked.

"Oh, we talked about lots of different things," said Nancy carefully. "They've certainly cleared up some of my questions. I'd still like to ask you a couple of things, though, if that's okay."

"What things?" asked Laurel suspiciously.

"Why don't you come in and sit down?" Nancy said. "It can't be very comfortable leaning against that wall."

Laurel walked in reluctantly and sat down on Lisa's bed. "What did you want to ask me?" she repeated.

Nancy smiled kindly. "This may be hard to talk about, Laurel. But I've been wondering whether you're jealous of Lisa for some reason."

"Jealous?" For a second Laurel looked as though she were about to deny it. Then, to Nancy's relief, she sighed. "Does it show that much?" she said. She stared at the floor. "I might as well confess. The truth is, I'm terrified that you and Ned might change Lisa's mind about working for Dad."

"And that would make things difficult for you," Nancy said slowly.

Laurel laughed bitterly. "Oh, everyone knows Lisa is Dad's favorite. It's no secret that he wants her to take over the business someday. And where will that leave me? Working for my younger sister? I'd always be second-best."

Nancy couldn't help feeling sorry for Laurel, but she knew she couldn't let pity cloud her judgment. Laurel appeared to have genuine reasons for resenting Lisa. The question was, how far did her grudge against her sister go? Far enough to puncture a tire? Far enough to set fire to Franklin Place and frame Lisa?

As to the puncture, Nancy thought, Laurel was just as strong a suspect as Lisa. And only a few people knew she and Ned were planning to visit Richard Bates today—and which car they'd be taking.

Suddenly, Nancy realized that Laurel might not even know about the puncture. She described what had happened on the way to San Rafael that morning. "You wouldn't know anything about that, would you?" she asked, watching Laurel's face.

Laurel looked pained. "I'm certainly not jealous enough of Lisa to puncture her tire, if that's what you mean. I didn't have anything to do with *that*." She broke off to check her watch. "Oh! I've got to get going," she said in a startled voice. "I'm expecting a call. Here, let me take your tray." And she was out the bedroom door in a matter of seconds.

A few moments later Ned knocked on the door. "I saw Laurel running away," he said. "Is it okay for me to come in?"

Nancy gave him a weak smile. "Sure. At least I know I can always trust you. At this point, Ned, I don't know who else I can trust in this house."

"Me neither," admitted Ned, sitting down in a chair.

"If I believe Lisa and Richard when they say neither of them set the fire, then what are they trying so hard to hide now? If I believe Laurel when she says she didn't puncture the tire, then that means Lisa did puncture it. That puts me right back where I started from."

"Just one big happy family, I guess," said Ned.

"Mmm." Nancy gazed at Ned with tired eyes. "We've been working on this case pretty hard, Ned. We're no closer to solving it now than we were when we started. If anything, we're even further away from solving it than we were yesterday. Instead of one suspect, we've got three. And the more we learn, the more confused I get."

Nancy sighed. "I'm starting to think we're just wasting our time."

9

The Night Strangler

Just then there was a knock on the bedroom door. Mr. Franklin poked his head into the room. Christopher Toomey was right behind him.

"May we come in?" asked Mr. Franklin.

"Of course," Nancy said.

"We've just come home from work," Mr. Franklin said. "Laurel told us about your accident the minute we walked in the door. I hope you're feeling better now."

"Much better, thank you," said Nancy.

Mr. Franklin was frowning. "I don't like that Bates boy at all," he said. "Laurel didn't say much, of course, but I gathered he was responsible for your fall. Am I right?"

Nancy exchanged a quick look with Ned. Richard Bates *was* a suspect—but even so, she couldn't really blame him for her fall. And on the chance that he *wasn't* guilty, it seemed too unfair to him and Lisa to turn Mr. Franklin even more strongly against him.

"Richard had nothing to do with it," Nancy told Mr. Franklin. "It was an accident. But I've been wondering," she added quickly. "You're an important man, Mr. Franklin. Is it possible that you have some enemies who might have set fire to the building?"

Mr. Franklin gazed uneasily at Mr. Toomey.

"If there *is* someone, please don't try to hide it," Nancy told them. "You can trust me and Ned."

"Well . . ." Mr. Toomey hesitated. "I hate to—"

"No, it's all right. Go ahead," his boss urged him.

"Well, there's Jake Ledwell," Mr. Toomey said slowly.

"Who's that?" asked Nancy.

"He's what's called a contractor," Mr. Toomey explained. "If he had worked for us, he would have hired men for the construction crew and brought building materials to the site. But his estimates were too high. We gave the job to someone else."

"Ledwell worked for me plenty of times in the past," Mr. Franklin added. "He always did a fine job. He would have made a lot of money on Franklin Place. But when he jacked up his prices sky-high, I couldn't possibly hire him."

"A good reason for Ledwell to be angry," Nancy said thoughtfully.

Mr. Toomey shook his head. "Ledwell was angry, all right, but he's no criminal. No, it couldn't be Ledwell. He has too much to lose."

He smiled at Nancy. "Not that I'm trying to do your job for you," he said.

Nancy smiled back. At least there was *one* cheerful person in this house, she thought.

"I think I should probably talk to Mr. Ledwell anyway," she said. "I'll give him a call tomorrow."

Just then Laurel appeared at the door. "The doctor is here," she said. "We'll have dinner right after he's seen you."

Nancy brightened. "If it's okay with the doctor, I'd like to have dinner downstairs. I really don't want to lie in bed all evening." Besides, she thought, she'd get more information on the case downstairs than she would up in Lisa's bedroom.

Half an hour later she walked into the dining room. She had changed into clean clothes—Mrs. Truitt had kindly washed the pants and shirt she'd worn to the fire—and was feeling a hundred percent better.

Richard Bates wasn't there, Nancy noticed, but all of the Franklins and Mr. Toomey were sitting in the same places they'd had the night before.

Everyone was very quiet at dinner. When the

92

meal was over, Mr. Franklin announced, "Laurel, Christopher, and I would like to take our coffee into the library for a brief work session. Is that all right with everyone else?"

"Fine, Uncle Bob," said Ned.

"Lisa, since you say you've quit, you may not wish to join us," her father told her. "However, you're welcome to come along if you want."

Lisa shrugged. "Might as well."

"Nancy and Ned, you're welcome to join us, too," Mr. Franklin said. "But you might rather have your coffee in here. We won't be long."

"Somehow I bet the two of you have had enough architecture for one day," Mr. Toomey said with a laugh.

"I think we *will* stay in here," said Nancy. "And I may need just a smidgen more of that delicious chocolate cake." She grinned. "After all, I'm an invalid."

Nancy and Ned were still relaxing in the dining room when Mr. Franklin's voice boomed out so loudly that they had no trouble hearing him.

"How could such a thing have happened?"

Then Laurel's voice rang out in dismay. "I—I don't know. How could I have? Oh, this is terrible!"

"We'd better go see what's up," Nancy told Ned.

In the library they found Laurel staring at some

93

blueprints. Her face was white with horror. Mr. Franklin was pale, too, and Mr. Toomey looked very shaken. Lisa stood a little distance away from them. She was biting her lip, but otherwise she seemed composed.

"What happened?" Ned said.

Laurel sank into a chair. "This is terrible," she moaned.

"It certainly is," her father said sternly. He turned to Nancy and Ned. "We've been going over our plans for Franklin Place," he explained. "We'll be rebuilding it, of course, and I was thinking about making some changes. Well, we found a mistake in our original calculations. The building was unsafe. It would have collapsed under its own weight!"

Laurel looked up. Her face was streaked with tears. "Why don't you just say it?" she demanded. "It was *my* mistake. I made those calculations. If it hadn't burned down, the building might have collapsed. People could have been killed!"

Lisa stepped toward her sister as if she wanted to comfort her, but Laurel pulled away.

"Don't tell me you're sorry!" Laurel cried. "I know what you're thinking, Lisa. If *you* had done the calculations, it wouldn't have happened!" She burst into fresh tears.

Nancy reached into her pocket for a tissue, but as

she pulled out her hand, something fell onto the carpet. It was the long piece of string she had found with Lisa's bracelet at the construction site. She stooped to pick it up.

As she straightened, she caught Mr. Toomey's eye. "Do you collect string, Nancy?" he asked with a smile.

"Not really," she answered. "I just happened to have some on hand."

"Oh, this is awful," Laurel wailed as she dabbed at her eyes.

"In a way it's a good thing, too," said Lisa.

Everyone turned to stare at her.

Lisa flushed. "I mean, since the building burned down, no one will ever know about the mistake. And no one will be hurt, either."

Laurel jumped to her feet. "You think *I* set the fire!" she cried. "You think I wanted to cover up my mistake!"

"No!" Lisa gasped. "No, that's not what I—"

"Well, you're wrong!" Laurel shouted. "You're all wrong!" She rushed out of the library.

Lisa shut her eyes tightly. "That's not what I meant," she whispered. Nancy could see that she was very upset. Mr. Toomey looked uncomfortable, but Mr. Franklin sank into the nearest chair, shaking his head in disbelief.

When he looked up, Nancy saw there were tears in his eyes. "You don't think she could have done it, do you?" he asked beseechingly.

"No!" Lisa cried out in dismay. "Don't even say that, Dad! Laurel could *never* have burned down Franklin Place!"

"I hope you're right." Mr. Franklin sounded like a beaten man.

Nancy walked up and put a hand on his shoulder. Her voice was firm. "Please, Mr. Franklin, don't worry," she said. "First thing tomorrow, Ned and I will pay a visit to Jake Ledwell. For now he's our prime suspect."

Nancy didn't add that there were still lots of unanswered questions about both of Mr. Franklin's daughters. She didn't want to stir up even more family trouble.

"I think I should probably go to bed," Nancy added. "I'm still pretty sore, and I could use the extra rest."

"I'll be up in a little while," Lisa told her tonelessly. "I'll stick around with Dad for a while."

"Thank you, Lisa," Mr. Franklin murmured.

Nancy couldn't help wincing a little as she headed out of the room. Ned was right behind her. "I'll help you up the stairs, Nancy," he offered.

When they reached Lisa's bedroom door, he whispered, "So what do you really think?"

Nancy sighed. "I didn't want to say anything to upset Mr. Franklin more, but Laurel just became a real suspect. We have to work fast, Ned—before this whole family falls apart." She sighed. "I have absolutely no idea who set the fire."

"Well, I believe Lisa and Laurel," Ned declared. "I'm positive they're both innocent."

"I hope you're right," Nancy said quietly.

Tired as she was, Nancy didn't fall asleep right away. She was still awake when Lisa came quietly into the room.

"Lisa, I have to ask you something," she said.

Lisa seemed startled. "I thought you were still asleep! What do you want to ask me?"

Nancy propped herself up on one elbow. "I couldn't help noticing that you didn't seem very surprised about those calculations. You knew before tonight that they were wrong, didn't you?"

Even in the dim light Lisa looked shocked. "How did you know?" she blurted out. Then she sighed and sat down on the edge of her bed. "I guess I just gave myself away," she said tiredly.

"Yes, I knew. I found out a while back when I was going over the plans. I guess I couldn't bring myself to say anything until it was too late. The longer I put it off, the more work was done on Franklin Place, and then it was even harder to say anything. It was a horrible feeling."

"But you finally decided to do something?" Nancy asked gently.

Lisa nodded. "Yes. I decided to destroy the calculations completely. That way, if anything happened, at least Laurel wouldn't get the blame. Not from the outside world, anyway.

"The night of the fire," Lisa went on, "I went over to Franklin Place, but the night watchman saw me. I checked out and came home."

Nancy frowned slightly. "I guess I don't understand why—"

"Why I would protect Laurel?" Tears filled Lisa's eyes. "I know Laurel is jealous of me," she said. "But she's still my sister. I don't want her to go to jail!"

"Why would Laurel go to jail?" asked Nancy.

Lisa stared at her in astonishment. "Why, for arson. Laurel must have tried to cover up her mistake."

She gave Nancy a bleak stare. "So what are you going to do now?"

"I don't know," Nancy told her honestly. "I guess the only thing *both* of us should do now is get some rest. We can talk about this some more in the morning, Lisa. And thanks for telling me."

Once Lisa was in bed, she fell asleep quickly.

Nancy stayed awake a little longer. She wanted to think about this new development in the case.

She certainly had more reason now to believe that Lisa didn't set the fire. In fact, now Lisa had a reason for staying silent about what she was doing at the site. But it didn't quite let her off the hook— and it didn't clear things up for Richard, either. Or for Laurel.

At the moment it seemed most likely to Nancy that Laurel had set the fire. If she had discovered her flawed calculations, would Laurel have had the strength to admit to her father what she'd done? Somehow Nancy could more readily imagine Laurel burning down Franklin Place than confessing her mistake to the father she so wanted to please.

Nancy stretched out on her side. She was starting to feel sleepy now.

I can think more about this in the morning, she thought drowsily.

It must have been a couple of hours later that someone shook Nancy roughly out of her deep, dreamless sleep. For a moment, as Nancy struggled to wake up, she thought she heard a strange, evil voice whispering to her.

"Where is it? Where is it?" the voice seemed to say.

Nancy couldn't answer. She had an odd sensation

in her throat. As she became more wide awake, she realized dimly that the room was dark except for a tiny glow of moonlight at the window. And someone was standing by her bed.

Suddenly Nancy was fully conscious. The voice hadn't been a dream. It was real! A dark, masked figure was leaning over her, hissing something incomprehensible into her ear.

Nancy felt a scream rise in her throat, but no sound escaped her lips. A pair of strong hands was tightening around her neck—and relentlessly squeezing the life out of her!

10

A Puzzling Question

Nancy struggled desperately to free herself, but the murderous hands only closed tighter around her neck. Spots were dancing in front of her eyes. She was beginning to feel faint. I've got to think of something, she told herself dizzily.

The lamp! It was right next to her bed. Wildly, Nancy threw out her arm and knocked the lamp to the floor.

There was a loud crash of breaking glass. In the other bed, Lisa sat up. "What was that?" she gasped.

Then she saw Nancy struggling with the masked intruder.

Lisa's scream ripped the air as she rushed to Nancy's side. "Help!" Lisa shrieked. "Someone, help us!"

She threw herself at Nancy's attacker, trying to

pull him away. But the intruder threw Lisa aside as if she weighed nothing at all.

His mask! Nancy thought. Get it off! Her lungs felt as though they were about to burst. She clawed frantically at her assailant's face. She couldn't get a firm grip on him, but her fingernails raked across his cheek. Finally, a corner of the mask came loose.

The intruder jumped back in alarm, pressing the mask to his face. Nancy took a huge breath of air. Then she joined her screams with Lisa's.

Footsteps pounded down the hall, and voices shouted. Without a moment's hesitation the intruder threw himself out the open window.

An instant later the bedroom door was flung wide open. The light flashed on overhead, and Ned rushed in, followed by Laurel and Mr. Franklin.

Ned ran straight to Nancy. "What happened? Are you all right?" he cried.

"I'm fine," Nancy managed to say. "Check the window! He got out that way!"

Mr. Franklin ran to the window. "No sign of anyone out there," he said. "Whoever it was got away fast. Lisa, what happened? Are you hurt?"

"I'm fine, Dad," said Lisa shakily. "But look at this room. Whoever that was, what did he want?"

Nancy looked around. The entire room had been torn apart. Drawers had been pulled open and rifled. Clothes had been tossed out of Lisa's closet and onto the floor.

"He was looking for something," Nancy said. "But who could it have been?"

"Isn't that clear?" said Mr. Franklin angrily. "Who *could* it be but Richard Bates? First he ran when he saw Nancy. Then he pushed her down the stairs. I've had enough!" he burst out. "I'm calling the police and having him arrested!"

"Dad, no!" shrieked Lisa. "You can't do that! It wasn't Richard! It couldn't possibly have been Richard!"

"Even if it *was* Richard," Nancy put in quietly, "you don't have enough evidence to have him arrested, Mr. Franklin. I do agree that you should call the police, though. Maybe they could check the room for fingerprints." She shuddered. "Though from the feel of that guy's hands on my neck, I think he was wearing gloves."

"This is getting too dangerous," Ned said fiercely. "I don't like it, Nancy!"

"It *is* getting more dangerous," Nancy said. "But that means we're getting closer to an answer. Someone really wants me off this case."

But what had the masked intruder been looking for? All Nancy could think of was Lisa's bracelet that she had found at the construction site. And why would anyone want that?

"Are you all right, Nancy?" Laurel asked. Nancy realized that everyone in the room was staring at her.

"I'm fine," she answered. "But maybe, since we're all okay, we should go back to bed. Do you have a dustpan so I can clean up that lamp I broke?" she asked Laurel.

"I'll do it," Laurel offered. "You stay in bed, Nancy. You've had a busy enough day already."

"I don't think 'busy' describes it," said Ned dryly.

When Nancy woke up, she felt a little stiff. After a shower and some breakfast, though, she was eager to get started.

"Are you still game for meeting with that contractor, Jake Ledwell?" she asked Ned. He was glancing through the sports section of the paper.

"Sure," Ned answered. "But what exactly are we going to say to the guy?"

"I was thinking about that in the shower," Nancy said. "And I've got a plan."

Nancy filled Ned in on the way to Ledwell Builders Associates, which was on the top floor of an old office building. As Nancy and Ned got out of the elevator, they could hear a man's voice yelling.

Nancy knocked on the office door, but the shouting didn't stop. She pushed the door open. Behind a large desk was a swarthy, muscular man talking on the telephone. A nameplate on the desk identified him as Jake Ledwell. A cigar was clenched firmly in his teeth. He glanced up for a second as Nancy and Ned walked into his office but made no sign that he had seen them.

"I gave you the lowest prices in town," he shouted into the phone. "I can't do better than that!"

He listened impatiently to the person on the other end. Then he slammed down the receiver and glared at Nancy and Ned.

"What are you two staring at?" he said crossly.

Nancy put on a bright smile and walked up to Mr. Ledwell's desk.

"Mr. Ledwell, I hear you're one of the best builders in town," she said sweetly.

"That's right. Now, if you kids don't mind, get right to the point. I don't have a lot of time to waste."

Nancy's smile didn't waver. "Well, I know we look young, Mr. Ledwell," she said, "but we're here to represent my father. I'm Nancy Drew, and this is Ned Nickerson. We both work for my father, Carson Drew. You may have heard of him. He's very big in real estate."

"Can't be that big. *I* haven't heard of him," Mr. Ledwell said grumpily. But he seemed to be paying attention now.

"That's because he usually works out of River Heights," Nancy explained. "But he's recently bought property here in San Francisco."

"And?" Mr. Ledwell was definitely starting to look interested.

"My father wants to put a luxury apartment building on his property," Nancy went on. "But— well—I'm afraid he might change his mind because of the misunderstanding."

"What misunderstanding?" Mr. Ledwell said, puzzled.

Nancy put on a look of wide-eyed innocence. "Well, my father heard such wonderful things about you that he's sure only you could handle this job."

"I don't have all day!" growled Mr. Ledwell.

"That's exactly how my father felt," Nancy said. "He's not a very patient man, to tell you the truth. And he didn't have all day, either. He called and called your office, but no one ever answered the phone."

Now Mr. Ledwell looked embarrassed. "Well, I, uh, had to fire my secretary last week," he said. "I guess I may have been a little hard to reach."

Nancy nodded. "Anyway, when he couldn't

reach you, my father decided to find another contractor."

"That's right," Ned added. "Mr. Drew was very disappointed, but he couldn't wait any longer."

"He shouldn't have given up so fast," Mr. Ledwell protested. "I'm the best!"

"My father tried to reach you again on the day before yesterday," Nancy continued. The day someone set fire to Franklin Place, she added silently.

Mr. Ledwell frowned. "That's the day I went to the bank, I think." He gave Nancy a weak smile. "My business has been a little short of cash lately."

"Maybe if I tell my father where you were, and that you couldn't get away, he just might give you another chance."

Mr. Ledwell pushed a large appointment book across the desk to her without a word. He's certainly more cooperative now, Nancy thought as she studied the page. He thinks there's big money in it for him.

"I see," she said aloud. "An afternoon appointment with a Mr. Casey."

"Went on for several hours," Mr. Ledwell said.

"And Mr. Casey will confirm that?" Nancy prodded.

"Sure. But you know, your father sounds like an awfully hard man to deal with," said Mr. Ledwell.

"Can't you give me his number and let me call him myself?"

Nancy hadn't planned on that.

"Of course," she said. "Here it is." She jotted down the number on a piece of paper. "He's in River Heights this week, so you'll have to call him there."

"No problem," said Mr. Ledwell. This time he actually sounded cordial. "Thank you, Miss Drew."

"What if he really calls your father?" Ned asked once he and Nancy were safely in the elevator.

Nancy grinned. "Dad's out of town on business. I'll have plenty of time to warn him."

"Did you hear the guy talking about being short of cash?" Ned asked as they reached the ground floor.

"I sure did," Nancy replied. "That would make him even angrier with Mr. Franklin for not hiring him. But at least his alibi is easy to check. I'll call the bank and talk to Mr. Casey when we get home."

A half hour later Nancy put down the receiver thoughtfully. "I guess Mr. Ledwell doesn't have an alibi after all," she said. "Mr. Casey says the appointment ended around four. That would have given him plenty of time to get over to Franklin Place and set the fire. We can't cross Mr. Ledwell off the suspect list quite yet."

108

Nancy and Ned were in the kitchen, eating lunch. "Let's hear the list again," said Ned, taking a bite of his sandwich.

"Well, there are two lists, really. The people who might have set the fire, and the people who might have attacked me last night. Mr. Ledwell, Lisa, Laurel, and Richard all have motives for setting the fire. As for last night—well, I suppose the guy might have been Ledwell. It's hard to imagine what he could have been looking for in Lisa's room, though. The only other possibilities are Richard and Mr. Toomey. And why would either of them—"

Just then the door burst open, and Lisa and Richard rushed into the kitchen.

"Have you heard?" asked Lisa breathlessly.

"Heard about what?" Nancy said, puzzled.

"Do you remember the trailer?" Lisa asked. "The one we used as an office at the Franklin Place site?"

Nancy thought for a second. "I think so. It was off to one side."

"That's right," Lisa told her grimly. "It was. And someone just tried to burn it down!"

11

A Sudden Flight

"Another fire!" gasped Nancy. "When did it happen?"

"Just now," Richard said. "Mr. Franklin called to tell Lisa. We were out in the yard, studying."

"Was anyone hurt?" Ned asked.

Lisa shook her head. "No. Laurel was the only one there. My father was out having lunch with Mr. Toomey. Laurel must have stayed behind to do some extra work. Anyway, Dad said Laurel saw smoke coming from under the trailer and called the fire department."

"She must have been terrified," Nancy said.

"Absolutely," Lisa agreed. "I mean, we're still recovering from the first fire—and now this!"

"Lisa wanted to drive over there right away," Richard said. "But I made her stay here. People might say she set this fire, too."

"Good thinking," said Nancy. "By the way, Richard, how long have you been here?"

Richard stared at her. "All morning. You're not going to try to pin *this* one on me, are you?"

"Not as long as you and Lisa have alibis," Nancy assured him.

"Well, we do," said Lisa. "You can ask Mrs. Truitt. She's been right here the whole time, cleaning. And she doesn't approve of Richard, so she'd never lie for him."

Nancy nodded. "Fine."

"Well, at least *someone* believes us for once!" Richard said.

"And Dad and Mr. Toomey were in a restaurant, so they have alibis, too," Lisa added.

Ned frowned. "But what about Laurel?" he asked. "She was the only one at the site when the fire started."

The color drained from Lisa's face. "You don't mean—will people think *Laurel* set the fire?"

"They might," Nancy said gently.

"That's ridiculous!" Lisa cried.

Nancy and Ned exchanged a look. "Well, if she didn't set it, I'm sure we won't have much trouble proving it. Where is Laurel now, by the way?"

Lisa blinked. "Still at the trailer, I guess. Why?"

"I was just wondering," Nancy said. She turned to Ned. "I think we'd better get over to Franklin

Place. I want to check out what happened." She glanced at Lisa. "Would it be okay if we used your car?"

Lisa nodded. "Richard and I want to come along, too. I'd like to see what's going on as much as you do. And Dad might need me."

They all piled into Lisa's car and drove down to Franklin Place. When they got there they could see that the office trailer was still standing, but the outside of it was black with smoke. Several firefighters were poking through the dirt for clues as Mr. Franklin and Mr. Toomey watched. Nancy could imagine how hard a new setback like this must seem.

"Dad!" Lisa called.

Her father turned eagerly at the sound of her voice, but he frowned when he saw Richard. "What's *he* doing here?"

"We were studying at home," Lisa answered. "We're doing a project for school."

"They have cast-iron alibis as far as this fire is concerned," Nancy said quickly. "Mr. Franklin, could you please fill us in on what happened here?"

Mr. Franklin nodded. "The fire started under the trailer," he said. "I'll show you. Be careful," he added as he led them to the trailer. "The ground's pretty muddy here from the firehoses."

The group stepped carefully through the mud behind the long metal trailer. Nancy peeked in one of the windows. Inside, the trailer had four desks, two bookcases, and a set of file cabinets that Nancy assumed held blueprints and other papers.

"Not much to see, really," said Mr. Franklin. "Laurel said she had taken a break and was walking around the building site when she smelled smoke. She came running, but the flames were small, so she used the fire extinguisher. By the time the fire department came, the fire was almost out."

"The firefighters gave the place a pretty thorough going-over," added Mr. Toomey.

"May we see the inside of the trailer?" Nancy asked.

"Sure," Mr. Franklin answered. "But again, I don't think there's much to see."

Someone had placed a few sheets of cardboard in front of the trailer door, where the mud was the worst. Nancy and the others entered the office. Inside, everything looked fine, although the smell of smoke was strong.

Mr. Toomey hurried from window to window, sliding them open. Then he turned to Nancy.

"Whatever happened at your meeting with Jake Ledwell?" he asked. "I mean, if he set the first fire, he probably set this one, too."

"He's definitely a possibility for the first fire," she agreed. "He's got an alibi for this one, though. Ned and I were with him this morning at exactly the time the fire must have been set."

It was possible, of course, that Ledwell had been working with Laurel, but Nancy didn't mention that. She didn't want to hurt the Franklin family any more right now. Besides, she'd need proof first.

"Could I take a quick look at your desks?" she asked Mr. Franklin.

"Certainly," he answered.

Mr. Toomey grinned at Nancy. "Just don't judge anything by my messy desk."

Nancy laughed. "Don't worry. I understand messy desks—you should see my father's. By the way," she added casually, "where's Laurel?"

"Well, as you might expect, she was very upset by all this," Mr. Franklin answered. "I sent her right home."

"Home?" Lisa looked puzzled. "Laurel wasn't home."

"Our paths probably crossed," Ned said.

"I'll call and see," said Lisa, picking up the telephone on her father's desk. But after a few moments of conversation she shook her head and hung up. "Mrs. Truitt says Laurel's not there," she told them.

114

"We can talk to Laurel later," Nancy said. She glanced around the office one more time. "I don't see anything out of the ordinary here. Ned and I might as well go home."

"Look who's coming," Ned said grimly.

Nancy checked the window. "Uh-oh," she said. "I was wondering how long it would take the reporters to find out about this."

A man and woman were heading toward the trailer. Nancy remembered them from the first fire. Getting away wouldn't be easy.

"There they are! Inside the trailer!" the woman called to her companion when she spotted Nancy. "What's going on? Is Mr. Franklin in there?" she shouted at Nancy.

"I'm afraid I can't tell you anything," Nancy called back. Quickly, she slid the window shut. Ned did the same with the other windows, and Richard closed the trailer door.

"Oh, no," Lisa moaned. "I can't face all those questions again!"

"You won't have to," Nancy assured her. "I have a better idea. The reporters will recognize your Camaro, so why don't we take your father's car? Ned and I can drive you home and bring your father's car right back. Is that all right?" she asked, turning to Mr. Franklin. He nodded.

"That should get us away from the reporters,"

Nancy said. "And I'll also have a chance to talk to Laurel back at the house. Now, Mr. Franklin, I wonder if you could help us out with something?"

Quickly she explained what she wanted him to do, and he nodded again. "I don't want extra publicity any more than you do," he said to Lisa. She gave him a grateful smile.

Then Mr. Franklin opened the door. As everyone had expected, the two reporters rushed up to him. "I'll be glad to talk to you," he told them cordially. "Let me show you exactly where the fire started. If you'll just follow me—this way, please. We're all very shocked, of course, and—"

Still talking, he led the two reporters behind the trailer.

"Okay, let's get going," Nancy directed. "Ned, could you go and get Mr. Franklin's car?"

The instant Ned brought the car to the door, Nancy, Richard, and Lisa bolted for it. Lisa scrambled into the backseat and ducked down out of sight as the car headed away from the building site.

Ned glanced into the rearview mirror. "Uh-oh, they've spotted us," he said. "But it's too late now. We're out of here!"

Lisa giggled as she peeked out the rear window. "We fooled them!" she crowed.

"They'll be back," Nancy warned. "But you're safe for now."

At the Franklin house Ned pulled the car close to the kitchen door. Lisa dashed inside, and the others followed.

Mrs. Truitt was sliding a tray of cookies into the oven. "Am I glad to see you!" she said. "Some reporters were here, but I didn't tell them anything."

"Thanks," Lisa told her. "What did Laurel say?"

Mrs. Truitt frowned. "But, dear, I told you. Laurel isn't here."

Lisa looked alarmed. "Still? Where could she be?" She turned to Nancy. "What do you think, Nancy? Could she have had some kind of accident on the way home or something?"

"It's possible," Nancy said guardedly. "But I don't think that's what happened."

"Well, what *do* you—" Richard began.

"Lisa, do you think your father will mind if we don't take his car back right away?" Nancy interrupted. "We've got to look for Laurel. She may not be planning to show up here at all."

"But why wouldn't she come home?" asked Lisa in a bewildered voice.

"I know you don't like thinking about this, Lisa,

but Laurel is a very strong suspect in this case," said Nancy. "She could be guilty of committing arson—twice. Maybe she's hiding from us, or she might be in some kind of trouble. But if we don't find her soon and get her to tell us the truth, she may wind up in jail!"

12

Clue in Chinatown

"I'll help you look for Laurel," said Lisa instantly. "If she's in some kind of trouble, I want to help her."

"I think it'd be better if we split up," said Nancy. "Why don't Ned and I take your father's car, and you and Richard go in Richard's."

"Fine with me," said Richard. "Where do you think we should look?"

"Is there anyplace Laurel might go if she had something on her mind?" Ned asked Lisa.

His cousin thought for a moment. "I can think of two places," she said. "Chinatown, for one. Laurel spends a lot of time there, poking around. And Fisherman's Wharf is the other place she might go. A couple of years ago she spent the whole day there after her boyfriend broke up with her. I guess we could try both places. It's better than sitting around at home worrying, anyway."

"Okay, you two go to Chinatown," agreed Nancy. "Ned and I will head back to Franklin Place to see if we can find out anything more. Then maybe we'll try Fisherman's Wharf. Why don't you give me a call at Franklin Place in about half an hour?"

"Okay," said Lisa. "Let's get going."

Unfortunately, traffic on the way to Franklin Place was maddeningly slow. Nancy sighed in exasperation as, once again, a traffic light changed to red just as they pulled up to it. "This is driving me crazy," she said.

"We're doing the best we can," Ned said.

Nancy watched the light. "True. But I wonder what Laurel is up to. I had been thinking that she couldn't possibly have set the second fire. I mean, it would have made her too obvious a suspect. She was the only person at the site. But her disappearing this way . . ." Nancy's voice trailed away as the light turned green.

Finally, they reached Franklin Place. Ned parked the car, and he and Nancy walked over to the trailer.

Inside, Mr. Toomey was hard at work. He was leafing through a pile of papers in front of him and punching numbers into a calculator.

"Hello," he said cheerfully when he saw Nancy

and Ned. "I'm just reworking some of Laurel's calculations. Pretty soon, you know, we'll have to rebuild Franklin Place. *This* time there won't be any mistakes. I'm making sure of that."

"Right," said Ned distractedly. "Where's Uncle Bob? We've brought back his car."

"He went to a meeting," Toomey told them. "He took Lisa's car, so you might as well go on using his."

"Well, at least we'll be driving around in style," said Ned.

"Driving around?" echoed Mr. Toomey. "Are you finally getting to do some more sight-seeing?"

Nancy smiled ruefully. "I wish. What we're really doing is looking for Laurel. Let me call Mrs. Truitt and see if she's turned up by now."

But Laurel still hadn't come home. Nancy checked her watch. "Lisa should be calling any second," she said. "Do you mind if we wait in here for her call, Mr. Toomey?"

"Of course not," he replied. "I'm delighted to have some company. Here, let me show you what I've been working on."

He spread a sheet of calculations in front of them before Nancy could say anything. "It's a terrible shame about these mistakes," Mr. Toomey muttered almost to himself. "Laurel's so talented. It would be such a pity if she lost her nerve after this—"

121

Just then the phone rang. Nancy crossed over to Mr. Franklin's desk and picked it up.

"Nancy? It's Lisa. We've pretty much finished with Chinatown." She sounded frustrated. "It's crazy to look for someone this way. I mean, Laurel could be anywhere! Anyway, we thought we'd try Fisherman's Wharf next, but can we join up with you? We could cover more ground that way."

"Good idea," said Nancy. "Tell me where you are now. We'll meet you there in a few minutes." Quickly, she jotted down the address Lisa gave her.

"We'll be waiting for you," said Lisa. "Bye!"

"Wait!" said Nancy. "We don't know—"

But Lisa had already hung up.

"Can you tell us how to get to Chinatown?" Nancy asked Mr. Toomey. "We're meeting Lisa and Richard there and heading on to Fisherman's Wharf."

"Sure," he said. "Now, what would be the most scenic route?" he mused.

"Thanks, Mr. Toomey, but we have to get there fast," Nancy interrupted.

"I see," said Mr. Toomey. "Too bad, though. There are a lot of things you could see on the way if you— Oh, well. Since you're in a hurry, your best bet is the cable car. It's not far from here."

Carefully, he began writing down the directions.

Please hurry! Nancy wanted to say as she

watched him stop to think. Mr. Toomey frowned and rubbed his chin thoughtfully. Finally, he handed them their directions.

"Thank you so much!" Nancy said as she and Ned raced out.

"Which way do we go?" Nancy asked Ned when they reached the street.

"We go left at the next corner," said Ned. "Then catch a cable car in a few blocks."

After a few minutes they reached the cable car stop just as a cable car pulled up, its bell clanging loudly.

Nancy and Ned scrambled aboard.

Under different circumstances Nancy would have loved the ride. The cable car kept swooping up and down incredibly steep streets and swinging thrillingly around corners. Beautiful streets flashed by, but Nancy was too intent on catching up to Lisa and Richard to pay attention to the scenery.

Holding tightly to a pole with one hand, she took the directions from Ned. "That's odd," she said, frowning. "There's makeup on this paper."

Ned glanced at the tan streaks. "So?"

"I'm wearing only blusher," Nancy told him.

"Well, don't look at me," Ned joked.

Nancy laughed, then looked at the directions again.

"Wait a minute," she said. "According to this, we

should already have passed Powell Street. We must have gotten on the wrong car."

She turned to a slender young woman standing beside them and showed her the slip of paper. "Excuse me, but have we missed our connecting stop?" she asked.

The woman glanced at the directions. "Oh, you can't get to Chinatown that way," she said.

Nancy looked at Ned in alarm. "But we *have* to get there!" she cried. "It's very important!"

The woman was clearly startled. "I do know a shortcut if you're really in a hurry," she said. "You'll get there as fast as a cable car would— maybe even faster."

She gave Ned and Nancy new directions. Nancy called out their thanks as she and Ned jumped off at the next stop. Then they ran down the crowded sidewalk as fast as they could.

"I hope *these* directions are right," Ned panted.

"They'd better be," said Nancy tersely.

After that they ran in silence, except for an occasional "excuse me" as one of them dodged a passerby. At last Nancy spotted the golden dragon that stood atop the huge archway crossing Grant Avenue.

"Chinatown," she said. "Finally!"

They raced two more blocks toward their destination, but there was no sign of Lisa or Richard.

Nancy and Ned stopped in front of a row of stores. Huge bins, filled with all kinds of merchandise, took up most of the sidewalk. Boxes of socks and sandals spilled over onto boxes of stuffed rabbits and tiny flashlights. There were pots and pans, coloring books, and jewelry all jumbled together.

"Look, Nan." Ned pointed to a telephone booth. It was painted bright red and trimmed with gold, with a fancy peaked roof made to look like a Chinese temple. "Maybe they called from there."

"Maybe," Nancy agreed. "But where are they now? They could have gone into one of the stores while they were waiting. Let's check the block."

"Fine," Ned said. "I'll look across the street." He began stepping through the busy traffic. Nancy hurried to the opposite corner and retraced her steps. There was still no sign of Lisa or Richard.

What could have happened? Nancy stopped to gather her thoughts as a man walked up to her, hissing to get her attention. When Nancy glanced his way, he held out a cardboard box. It was filled with brightly colored tubes.

"Firecrackers," the man whispered. "Left over from Chinese New Year's. I'll give you a good price."

Nancy frowned. "No, thanks."

"They're not dangerous," the man said coaxingly. "See?"

He lifted a red firecracker and waved it in front of Nancy's face. A long string dangled from one end.

"See," the man told her. "Extra-long fuse. Plenty of time to get away—then, BANG!"

Nancy jumped back, startled. The man threw back his head and howled with loud, high-pitched laughter.

"Nan! Over here!" Ned called from the corner. He was waving wildly, and Lisa and Richard were with him.

Filled with relief, Nancy hurried toward the others.

"Sorry," Lisa said as Nancy ran up. "We were waiting in a store. Who was that man you were talking to?"

Nancy made a face. "He wanted to sell me firecrackers with an extra-long fuse."

"Firecrackers!" said Ned in amazement. He took Nancy's arm, and they began walking quickly along behind Lisa and Richard. "What made him think you'd be interested in firecrackers? He must be trying to unload them before anyone can—"

Suddenly, Nancy froze. "Ned! That's it!" she gasped.

Everyone stared at her. "*What's* it?" asked Richard.

"The firecrackers!" Nancy cried. "I know who set the fire! And I know how!"

13

Racing Toward Danger

Lisa, Richard, and Ned were staring at Nancy as though she'd gone crazy. "I just figured it out!" she said. "It's so obvious, once you look at it the right way."

"What's obvious, Nancy?" asked Ned. "Who are you talking about?"

"The one person none of us ever suspected," Nancy said with a sigh. "Christopher Toomey."

"Toomey!" Ned looked astonished. "But that's—"

"Christopher couldn't have set the fire," Lisa said, frowning. "He was at our house when the first fire started, and with Dad for the second one. Besides, he's practically one of the family."

Nancy smiled wryly. "I know. That's why I put everything together only this minute. You see, I forgot one of the most important things about being a detective."

"What's that?" asked Richard.

"That sometimes you have to look in the most obvious places," Nancy replied.

Lisa shook her head slowly. "But what about his alibi?"

"Well, he was very clever," Nancy replied. "But it was all a trick."

"So how did you figure it out?" asked Richard.

Nancy smiled. "Well, two things tipped me off. For one thing, Toomey is wearing makeup today."

Ned stared at her in disbelief.

"Uh-huh." Nancy showed Lisa and Richard the piece of paper on which Toomey had written directions to Chinatown. She pointed to the tan streaks.

"I'm not wearing foundation," she explained, "and this was a clean piece of paper from Toomey's notepad. Obviously, Toomey was the one wearing the makeup. I scratched someone's face when I was attacked last night."

Nancy motioned across the street. "And then I saw those firecrackers. They provided the other clue I needed. You see, they had extra-long fuses—long strings, like the one I found with Lisa's bracelet at the construction site. Toomey must have set the fire with a timer attached to an explosive. That device gave him all the time he needed to plant his bomb and get away from Franklin Place. He could have set today's fire that way, too. He was probably hoping to frame Laurel and scare her half to death at the same time."

"You mean it was all set up in advance?" Ned asked.

"That's right," Nancy answered. "The night of the first fire, Toomey must have set the timer, then left to pick us up at the airport. Then he drove us back to the Franklins' house for dinner. About the time we finished dinner, the timer went off and the explosives blew up, starting a huge fire. No one suspected Toomey because he was with us the whole time. We were his alibi."

"But anyone could have used the same device," Ned objected. "Like Laurel, for instance."

"That's true. But remember that night in the study, when Laurel discovered the mistakes she'd made in the calculations? I offered her a handkerchief. The string I'd picked up on the site fell out of my pocket. I remember now that Toomey stared at it. He must have panicked because he knew what it was."

"And he was afraid you'd figure out that the string was an explosive's fuse," Ned said. "And then you'd realize that the arsonist didn't have to be at Franklin Place to set the fire."

"Exactly," Nancy said. "Toomey broke into Lisa's

room that night, looking for the string, but he couldn't find it. I thought it was Lisa who was walking around the room. He came back the next night but still couldn't find the string. That's when he got angry and went after me."

"I still can't believe it," said Lisa. "Christopher!"

"I've got to hand it to you, Nan," Ned said, shaking his head. "You're one smart detective. You figured it all out from a piece of string."

"Yes, but it took me a long time," Nancy said.

"So Christopher must have been happy when everyone suspected me, right?" asked Lisa. "And after the fire under the trailer, people would think *Laurel* was guilty."

"Probably," said Nancy. "I'm sure he thought no one would ever suspect *him.*"

Lisa shuddered. "What a terrible story. Wait till my father hears this."

"There's more," Nancy told her. "But right now we'd better get to Richard's car. I just realized something else—we've got to get to Fisherman's Wharf fast. Laurel may be in danger."

"But why?" asked Lisa in horror.

"There's no time to explain now," Nancy said gravely. "We've spent way too much time talking here already. I'll tell you guys everything on the way to Fisherman's Wharf, okay?"

Richard led them quickly to his beat-up old car,

and they all piled in. But the streets were a snarled mess of traffic.

"We'll never get anywhere at this rate," Lisa said anxiously.

"I'll try another route." Richard swung the wheel and turned down a narrow side street. The traffic was somewhat thinner there, but they still couldn't move as fast as Nancy would have liked.

Lisa turned around in the front seat. "Nancy, I still don't understand why you think Laurel is in trouble."

Nancy took a deep breath. "This is the way I see it," she began slowly. "Toomey has worked for your father for many years. For so long, in fact, that everyone takes him for granted. He's spent a lot of time with the family, run errands, *and* worked at the firm. When Laurel began working for your father, it would have been logical to expect that she'd start doing more of the clerical stuff and the errands. But instead, she started straight on architectural work. Toomey must have been jealous."

Lisa nodded. "I can definitely see that."

"He put up a good front, though," Nancy said. "He sure had me fooled for a while."

"But Laurel is so much younger and so much less experienced as an architect," said Ned. "She's only starting out. How could Toomey be that jealous?"

"She was catching up," Nancy pointed out.

"Your uncle kept talking about Laurel and Lisa working for him. He rarely even mentioned Toomey. It must have embarrassed Toomey to be picking up people at airports while someone who was a lot younger was working so closely with his boss."

The light turned green, and Richard zoomed the car forward. Lisa looked thoughtful. "We all treated him pretty badly, didn't we? I didn't even realize it."

"And things must have gotten worse when *you* went to work for your father," Nancy continued. "He kept talking about how proud he was of you. He even announced that you'd be his partner someday. And that was the job Toomey had always wanted. He was so furious that he decided to get even with everyone—by destroying the family's most important project."

"Franklin Place," Lisa murmured.

"He must be nuts!" Ned said.

"I think you're right," said Nancy with a shiver. "I wish I'd seen earlier that Toomey was the only person who had a real motive for revenge. Once Franklin Place was destroyed, he probably would have run off—except that you quit your job, Lisa. He must have been delighted—and even more delighted when Laurel's mistakes were discovered.

He may have thought she'd quit, too, or even get fired. And with both of you gone, he would have a shot at running the firm after all."

"But Dad would never fire Laurel," Lisa said. "She made a terrible mistake, but she's only a beginner. Toomey should have spotted the mistake."

"That's true," Nancy agreed. "But either way, Toomey must have thought the mistake gave him his big chance to impress your father. He went right to work redoing the calculations to prove he could do the job."

"He *is* crazy," Ned muttered. "You know, Nan, he *did* sound kind of creepy in the trailer today. Remember how he said there wouldn't be any more mistakes? There was something weird in his voice."

"I thought so, too," Nancy agreed. "He seemed different somehow. It sort of jarred me—and once I saw the makeup and the firecrackers, everything fell into place."

"But why do you think Laurel is in danger now?" asked Richard.

"I hope I'm wrong," said Nancy worriedly. "But I don't think so. Toomey doesn't think you're a threat anymore, Lisa, now that you've quit. But he gave me and Ned the wrong directions to China-town. He *wanted* us to get there late. That may

133

mean he's trying to beat us to Fisherman's Wharf. He wants to find Laurel before we do. I think he'll do anything at this point to get her out of his way."

Lisa gasped. "Then Laurel really is in danger! Oh, Nancy, we've got to help her!"

Just then Richard pulled into a parking spot. "We're here," he announced in a relieved voice. "Finally!"

Through the window Nancy saw dozens of boats bobbing in the harbor at long piers. Modern fishing boats were anchored next to huge sight-seeing cruisers. Nancy could see why Fisherman's Wharf was a popular tourist area. People were streaming in and out of shops and restaurants and museums and crowding the streets near the waterfront. Some were flying kites and balloons; others were watching street performances.

But right now all Nancy could think about was how hard it would be to track Laurel down in the crowd.

Lisa was evidently having the same thought. "How will we ever find Laurel with all the people around?" she wailed as they piled out of the car.

"Where does she usually go?" Nancy asked.

"I'm not really sure." Lisa frowned. "We used to come here a lot together, but I haven't been back for years. She used to like the wax museum and the ship—"

134

"That ship?" Nancy turned and pointed to the old-fashioned square-rigger behind them. It loomed over the dock area, its tall masts soaring above their heads.

"That's the one," Lisa replied. "It's huge inside."

"Are we supposed to be looking for Laurel or Toomey?" asked Richard.

"We've got to look for both of them," Nancy answered. She turned to Lisa. "What was Laurel wearing today?"

"A green knit dress with a turtleneck," Lisa replied. "Kind of a blue-green."

"And Toomey was wearing a brown suit with a light blue shirt," Ned put in. "He might have taken off the jacket, though."

"Okay," said Nancy. "Now, if anyone spots Toomey, don't do anything foolish. He may be really desperate."

"What should we do if we see him, then?" Lisa asked.

"Just follow him," Nancy replied. "But try not to let him see you. Okay. Is everyone ready to start?"

Richard looked a little nervous.

"Not much could happen out in the open like this," Nancy assured him. "Let's split up. Lisa and Richard, you check the wax museum and the shops along the boardwalk. We'll meet back here in fifteen minutes."

Richard frowned. "What happens if we find Laurel?"

"Bring her back here and stay with her," Nancy answered. "Whatever you do, don't leave her alone. Not even for a minute."

Lisa and Richard nodded and hurried away.

"Maybe I should check the piers in the other direction," Ned suggested. "Laurel may be just strolling along, listening to the musicians or something. Where will you be?"

Nancy nodded. "I'll take the old ship," she told him.

"Well, good luck," said Ned, taking off down the pier.

"Good luck!" Nancy called after him.

Then she headed for the gangplank that led up to the old square-rigger.

Nancy bought a ticket, and the ticket taker waved her on irritably. "Tour's already started," he barked. "Go on, go on!"

Nancy hurried up to the wooden deck. It was littered with piles of old fishing nets, barrels, and boxes.

The tour guide was standing in front of a small group about twenty feet away. Nancy glanced around. Where should she start? On her right, she noticed a covered hatch that led into the ship.

She hurried down the narrow wooden steps and turned into the first room she found. Three tourists looked up curiously as Nancy burst in. "Where's the fire?" one of them asked.

"Sorry," said Nancy, rushing out of the room again.

Then up ahead Nancy saw a man wearing a blue shirt and brown pants disappear around the corner. Even in the dim light Nancy recognized Christopher Toomey instantly.

She darted toward him just as a group of middle-aged women emerged from a room ahead of her. Chattering and laughing, they moved slowly down the narrow hallway. By the time Nancy had threaded her way through them, Toomey was nowhere to be seen.

Nancy raced back up the stairs. Was Toomey on deck? For an instant she couldn't see anything at all. The sudden bright sunlight was hurting her eyes.

Then toward the rear of the ship Nancy spotted a flash of blue-green.

"Laurel!" she called urgently. "Wait!"

But as Nancy sprang forward, she caught her foot in a coil of fishing net. Down she went, face first, onto the deck.

Instantly, she pushed herself back onto her feet. Her knees stung terribly from the fall, but she couldn't think about that now. She gazed anxiously around the deck, but there was no sign of the blue-green dress.

Nancy groaned inwardly. How was she going to warn Laurel? She glanced at her watch and saw that the fifteen minutes had passed. Well, she couldn't go back to the others now. Not when she was this close. Besides—

Suddenly heavy footsteps sounded behind her. Before Nancy could move, a strong arm had grabbed her from behind.

Then a deep voice growled, "I've got you now, Nancy Drew!"

14

Overboard!

Before she could draw a breath to scream, Nancy felt herself being hoisted roughly toward the ship's railing. Then she was dangling above the cold waters of the bay.

Nancy heard someone yelling in alarm. We've been spotted! she thought with relief. But the hands never relaxed their hold.

"Thought you could stop me, didn't you?" Toomey's evil chuckle rang in her ear.

Then he hurled Nancy toward the water as easily as if she'd been a piece of driftwood.

Nancy felt an icy smack as she hit the water and plunged downward. She furiously clawed her way back up. Then she was bobbing, gasping, on the surface of the water. High above her, a voice shouted, "Girl overboard!"

There was another splash as something hit the water near Nancy.

It was the bottom of a rope ladder. Someone was scrambling down it toward her. Nancy swam quickly to the side of the ship just as the person climbing down dropped to the bottom of the ladder. In another second Nancy had grabbed his outstretched hand.

She pushed the dripping hair out of her eyes. "Richard!"

"Well, it was my fault you fell down Coit Tower," Richard said with a grin. "I owed you a rescue. Are you okay?"

"I'm fine," Nancy said through chattering teeth. "Just a little cold."

In fact, her fingers were so numb already that she had a hard time holding on to Richard. The deck of the ship seemed miles away. Sheets of water were pouring from her clothes, and her jeans and sweatshirt—heavy with water—were sticking to her. Nancy was racked with shivers. Suddenly her arms felt too weak to pull her up onto the ladder.

"You can do it," Richard urged. "One more try."

Somehow Nancy managed to haul herself up the first rung of the ladder. Then Richard reached down, grabbed her around the waist, and pulled her up beside him.

"You go first," he said. "I'll be right behind you."

It took all Nancy's strength to pull herself up the rope. Slowly she climbed, rung by rung, until finally she reached the ship's railing. Then Ned's strong arms were lifting her to the deck. Someone else ran up with a warm blanket, and Ned draped it around her.

"Th-th-thanks," Nancy stuttered. "And thanks to you, Richard, for the rescue." She looked around at the crowd of curious onlookers. "I'm okay," she said with a weak grin. "Thanks, everyone."

Then Nancy saw Lisa right behind Ned. And standing next to Lisa, her arm through her sister's, was—

"Laurel!" Nancy cried. "Where d-did you come from?"

"She was up on deck when we got here," said Lisa.

"That's right." Laurel nodded. "I was about to leave the ship when I heard that someone had fallen overboard. I ran to the railing, like everyone else. Lisa, Richard, and Ned were right behind me."

"Did they tell you what was going on?" asked Nancy.

"They sure did." Now Laurel shivered, too. "It's horrible, Nancy. I had no idea Christopher was involved in all of this. I had no idea how he felt about me, either."

"No one did," said Lisa soberly. She gave her sister a quick hug.

"Lisa, Richard, and I went back to the square when our fifteen minutes were up," Ned told her. "None of us had found Laurel. We waited another few minutes for you, Nancy. When you still didn't show up, I started to get worried. I thought you might be having trouble searching the whole ship. So we came to help."

Nancy gave them all a grateful look. "I'm awfully glad you came after me."

Then she paused to stare at the crowd on deck. The circle of onlookers around her had pretty much dispersed, but there were still dozens of people on the boat. "Where is Toomey now, anyway?" she asked.

"Gone," Ned said disgustedly. "He was running from the ship when we got here. I know I should have chased after him, but then I heard someone yelling 'Girl overboard.'"

"We didn't know who was in trouble—you or Laurel," Richard chimed in. "So we all raced up here. And, well, you know the rest."

"Thank goodness you *did* race up here," said Nancy. "And thank goodness Toomey didn't have time to get to Laurel."

Laurel took Nancy's hand and squeezed it.

"Thank *you*, Nancy. I still can't believe everything these guys told me. I really owe you a lot."

Ned was shaking his head. "I can't believe Toomey got away."

"Don't worry about that now, Ned," Nancy told him. "Lisa and Laurel are safe. That's what really matters."

"Hey, I just remembered something," Richard said. "I've got some extra clothes and a blanket in my car."

"Great!" Nancy said enthusiastically. She tugged at her clammy sweatshirt. "Anything would be better than this."

Richard hurried back to his car to get the clothes. The others stayed with Nancy. When Richard returned, Nancy went into the ladies' room on the ship. There she changed quickly and dried her hair with the blanket.

"Feeling better?" Ned asked when she came out.

"Much," Nancy said. "It's good to be dry again." She twirled around to show off her baggy black sweatpants and a huge sweatshirt with *San Rafael University* printed across the front. Everyone laughed.

"Listen," Nancy said, suddenly serious. "We can't waste any more time thinking about me. We have to go to the police and tell them about

Toomey. He knows we're on to him now. He has to be more desperate than ever. Now that he knows *we* know about him, he's got nothing to lose."

"Why don't we all walk Laurel to her car?" Ned suggested. "Then Nancy and I can go with her."

"Fine," Richard agreed, and the five of them walked quickly off the ship.

"It's in this direction," said Laurel, turning down a side street. "Boy, I'm glad I parked it here, out of the crowds. I'm in no shape to negotiate some of the busier streets right now."

But as she led them quickly along the sidewalk, Laurel suddenly stopped. "Look, there's a phone booth across the street," she said. "I'd better call Dad. He'll be wondering where we are."

"Good idea. And you'd better tell him about Toomey, too," said Nancy. "Your father should know that Toomey is dangerous."

"Right," said Laurel. She slipped her arm away from Lisa's and began crossing the street.

"Wait, Laurel!" Nancy called after her. "Let me come with you!"

There was a sudden loud clanging of bells as a cable car whipped around the corner. It was going so fast that Laurel had to leap out of its way. Nancy started after her.

"Watch it, Nan!" Ned said. He grabbed Nancy

and pulled her back to the curb. The cable car passed safely between them and Laurel.

"But, Ned," Nancy cried. "Laurel's on the other side of the street."

"It's okay," Ned said reassuringly. "She'll be there for only a minute."

It seemed to take much longer than that for the cable car to pass. Finally it was gone. Nancy looked anxiously across the street to the phone booth.

"Oh, no!" she gasped.

The door to the phone booth hung open. The booth was empty, and the receiver was swinging at the end of its cord.

Christopher Toomey was standing next to the booth. One of his hands was over Laurel's mouth, and the other was wrapped tightly around her waist. Laurel's eyes were wild with terror, and she was struggling desperately to get away.

"*Laurel!*" Lisa screamed. She started for the curb with Nancy, Ned, and Richard right behind her.

Toomey gave Laurel a vicious yank backward. "Don't come any closer!" he shouted. "Or it'll be the last time you ever see Laurel alive!"

15

Terror Trap

"I'm warning you!" Toomey yelled again. "Keep away, or I'll do something crazy!"

"He *is* crazy!" Ned muttered under his breath.

"Please, Christopher, don't hurt my sister!" Lisa begged. Tears were running down her cheeks.

I've got to do something, Nancy thought. But what?

Before she could collect her thoughts, Toomey pushed Laurel into the phone booth again. Then he stood in front of it, leaning against the door. "Don't any of you come over here," he growled. He glared over his shoulder at Laurel. "And don't you even *think* about making any calls, or I'll finish you off right here." Inside the phone booth Laurel collapsed in sobs.

"What do we do now?" Ned whispered to Nancy.

"I'm not sure—we don't know if he has a weapon. I don't think Toomey knows what to do, either." Nancy frowned a little, thinking rapidly.

"I have an idea," she said after a moment. "Can you keep Toomey talking for a while?"

"I'll try," Ned answered. "What are you going to do?"

"I'm going across the street," Nancy said quietly. "You keep Toomey's attention so he doesn't notice me. I'll try to sneak around and come up behind him."

"Then what?" quavered Lisa.

"Then I'll just have to think of something." Nancy squeezed Ned's arm and slipped behind him.

No one had been on the street when Toomey had grabbed Laurel, and the few people walking down the block now didn't seem to notice anything wrong. Toomey was leaning against the door of the phone booth as if he were waiting for Laurel to finish a phone call.

Nancy walked quickly down the sidewalk about twenty feet. When a minivan rumbled down the street, she waited until it pulled past her, then darted across the street behind it.

To her intense relief, a group of tourists was coming down the other side of the street. She walked as inconspicuously as possible into the middle of the group. Now there was little chance Toomey would spot her.

Suddenly one of the women stopped in front of a restaurant, next to a small alley. "This looks like a nice place," she said to her friends.

"It's fine with me," said one of her companions. Chattering happily, the group began walking into the restaurant.

Nancy walked in right along with them. If she didn't, Toomey would surely spot her. A couple of the women in the group looked curiously at her, but she ignored them. Then she made straight for the rest room sign. Maybe there would be another exit out of the restaurant that way.

The sign led her down a hall. At the end of the hall, past the telephone and the bathrooms, there *was* a door. It was halfway open, and Nancy could see it let out onto the alley.

She slipped out the door and tiptoed to the end of the alley, keeping flat against the wall of the restaurant. The telephone booth was straight ahead of her. Toomey was still leaning protectively against the door of the booth.

Nancy could see Lisa and Richard still on the other side of the street. Ned must have persuaded Toomey to talk to him because he had crossed the street and was now about ten feet from Toomey.

Nancy could just manage to hear what Ned was saying.

"You were very clever," Ned said admiringly. "That trick with the tire—smart." He edged ever so slightly closer to Toomey as he spoke.

"You figured that out, did you?" Toomey answered.

"Yes, but it took us a long time," said Ned.

"I'm impressed," said Toomey. "What else have you figured out?"

Ned inched closer. "Everything, I think," he said in a matter-of-fact voice. "But I'm not sure why you set those fires."

"You're not sure!" Toomey let out a strange, high-pitched laugh. "I'll tell you why. Because no one paid attention to me!" Now his laugh sounded more like a sob. "I'm the smartest one in that office, and no one would ever admit it!"

He's going off the deep end, Nancy realized. She'd have to move fast.

She tiptoed up to the very end of the alley and peeked out again. Toomey was ranting now, and Ned was listening with a sympathetic look on his face.

"Even Mr. Franklin never paid attention!" Toomey shouted. "I was practically like a son to him! And let me tell you—"

Nancy waved her hand to get Ned's attention. He noticed and gave a tiny nod. She motioned to him to get Toomey away from the phone booth.

Ned took a step to the right, frowning as if he were thinking hard.

"You know, you're right, Mr. Toomey," he said. "You *are* a smart man. I don't think my uncle appreciated that."

"That's what I'm trying to say!" Toomey exclaimed excitedly. He took a few steps toward Ned. "That's what I've been trying to say the whole time!"

Nancy picked up a little pebble from the edge of the sidewalk. She tossed it against the phone booth and Laurel looked up, startled.

Nancy put a finger to her lips, motioning to Laurel not to say anything.

Then she took a few careful steps toward the phone booth. Toomey was still deep into his conversation with Ned. He seemed to have forgotten all about Laurel.

Keeping a watchful eye on Toomey, Nancy sneaked toward the telephone booth.

"Now!" she yelled, hurling herself straight at Toomey. He fell like a sack of potatoes, with Nancy on top of him. Laurel yanked the door open, jumped over Toomey's fallen form, and raced across the street to her sister.

150

"No!" Toomey screamed as he saw Laurel escape. He shook Nancy off and struggled to his feet. Nancy grabbed him around the ankles, and Ned tackled him, bringing him down again.

This time he sprawled face first on the sidewalk. By now Richard had raced across the street.

Ned was holding Toomey down, and Richard pinned Toomey's arms behind his back. "Don't even think of going anywhere," Richard said.

Toomey twisted his head around and glared up at Nancy. His face was a contorted mask of anger and hatred. "I'll get you for this!" he said.

"I don't think so," Nancy answered. "I think you'll be going to jail."

Across the street Lisa had her arms around Laurel and was holding her tightly. Nancy smiled at them. Then she went to the phone booth and dialed the police.

Nancy settled back against the comfortable couch and sighed contentedly. After taking a long, hot bath, she had changed into fresh clothes and eaten a huge dinner. Now she was sitting with the Franklins, Ned, and Richard in the living room. Everyone was sipping coffee or hot chocolate, and at last everyone was relaxing.

Ned leaned toward Nancy and handed her a second cup of hot chocolate.

"You've got to build up your strength," he teased.

"You've certainly done a lot on our behalf," said Mr. Franklin seriously. "I can never thank you enough, Nancy."

"You don't have to thank me," Nancy replied. "I'm just glad we found out about Toomey before anyone got hurt."

"He was an awful man," Lisa said. "But I still can't help thinking what a sad story it is. Jealousy can be a terrible thing."

She turned to Laurel. "You know, there's room for two more architects in the Franklin family."

Laurel blushed. "I *was* pretty jealous," she admitted. "I don't blame you for being angry at me."

"I'm not angry at you," Lisa said. "I never was."

Laurel looked puzzled. "Then why *were* you so mad?" she asked.

"Because no one ever asked me what kind of work I wanted to do," Lisa replied. "But I did want to protect you, Laurel. I saw your mistakes a long time ago. I wanted to tell you about them, but you wouldn't give me a chance. And I was afraid to tell anyone else. I didn't know what to do. That's why I went to the site the night of the first fire. I was going to destroy the calculations."

"It's always better to admit your mistakes, no matter how bad they might seem," Mr. Franklin said.

"You're right about that, Dad," Laurel said.

"Well, we all make mistakes," Mr. Franklin said briskly. "The truth is, I've always been proud of both my daughters."

He patted Laurel's hand. "I gave you a lot of responsibility, Laurel. Maybe too much. But that was because I had so much faith in you. I should have told you that. And I will tell you, from now on."

"Then I can still work in the office?" Laurel asked timidly.

"Of course! I wouldn't have it any other way," her father insisted.

Suddenly Richard, who had been drinking his coffee in silence, spoke up from the sofa. "Sir, you'd be proud of Lisa's school project, too," he said. "She's got great ideas. You should see the model we made."

Mr. Franklin hesitated for a minute. "You're right," he said at last. "I *will* go and see it. All this trouble has made me realize that I've never appreciated Lisa's originality. It's about time I started picking up a few new ideas, even at my age. I'll drive out to San Rafael tomorrow and take a look."

Lisa beamed at him. "Fantastic! I know I've got a lot more to learn, too," she added. "But you and Laurel can help me."

"We will," Laurel and Mr. Franklin answered in unison. Everyone laughed.

In a few minutes the conversation turned to architecture, and the new designs for Franklin Place. Well, what would you expect? thought Nancy. With four architects in one room, it was probably impossible to avoid the subject.

Nancy reached for Ned's hand. "We never did get much of a vacation," she said quietly.

"Well, we still have a few days left," Ned said. "And starting tomorrow, I'm going to have a great vacation with the best detective I know!"

154